All of the Above

ESPECIALLY FOR GIRLS™ Presents

All of the Above

Christi Killien

Houghton Mifflin Company

Boston 1988

The author is grateful for permission to quote from
The Thirty-Six Dramatic Situations by Georges Polti.
Reprinted by permission of The Writer, Inc.

This book is a presentation of **Especially for Girls™**,
Weekly Reader Books. Weekly Reader Books offers
book clubs for children from preschool through high school.
For further information write to: **Weekly Reader Books,**
4343 Equity Drive, Columbus, Ohio 43228.

Published by arrangement with Houghton Mifflin Company.
Especially for Girls and Weekly Reader are trademarks of Field Publications.

Library of Congress Cataloging-in-Publication Data

Killien, Christi.
  All of the above.

  Summary: Fifteen-year-old MacBeth Langley falls head
over heels for the new boy at school and enlists her old
friend, the boy next door, to help her in her romantic
schemes.
  I. Title.
PZ7.K5564A1   1987   [Fic]   86-27872
ISBN 0-395-43023-2

Printed in the United States of America

For Janine

One

If there is one thing that I hate, it's being ordinary. And if there's another thing I hate, it's reading about ordinary people. I want my life to be packed full of adventure and romance, especially the latter. But around here in the summer, the pickings of both are slim.

I was just starting a new Agatha Christie mystery when the phone rang. I raced into my parents' room. It sounds strange, I know, but answering the phone is one of the more exciting things I've done this summer.

"Hello?" I said, breathlessly, hopefully, desperately.

"I'm back, MacBeth!" Antoinette Bigley-Barnes bubbled over the phone line. She had spent the summer in Japan.

"Hi, Antoinette!" I shrieked. "I was hoping it was you! I'm so glad you're back!"

"I can't wait to see you! Guess what? I got my hair cut! I learned *karate*! And I brought you *a present*!"

Silence. Was this the same Antoinette Bigley-Barnes that I'd known since our parochial school days? The same best friend who wore her long hair in pigtails and, for excitement, speculated with me about the secret personal lives of the nuns?

"Thanks," I finally said. "I'm glad you had a good time."

"Are you okay?" Antoinette asked softly, as if she suddenly realized how long and boring *my* summer had been, reading, doing housework, and seeing an occasional play with my mother, the playwright. My father's the one who named me Elizabeth Jane Langley; my mother's the one who dubbed me MacBeth, after the play by Shakespeare.

"I know I sent you only a couple of postcards . . ." Antoinette apologized.

"I'm fine," I assured her, feeling guilty for being sad. "What did you say about karate?"

"In Japan! My parents let me take karate lessons! And, oh, MacBeth, I met this boy named Yoshi! Can you believe it?"

"Believe what? That your parents gave you lessons, that you learned karate, or that you met a boy named Yoshi?" My voice sounded light and friendly, even though the weight of the twin imps, Envy and Melancholy, hung on the corners of my mouth.

Antoinette burst out laughing. "You're the same ol' MacBeth!"

"Yeah, I guess so." That's the problem, I thought. I'd endured an entire summer of boredom, but hearing this from Antoinette was the last straw. I *had* to get my life moving.

Antoinette laughed again. "Look. I'm going to teach you some karate. It's so simple, and it's fun!"

For a moment that sounded promising. And exciting.

But then I remembered who I was. MacBeth Langley, a stranger to harmonious physical movement.

Antoinette was there last year when Mr. Erlich, our ninth grade P.E. teacher, called me a perfect mesomorph in front of the entire class. It was during his Body Types lecture. Mesomorph means muscular and athletic, and Mr. Erlich was puzzled because I look like an athlete ("impeccable posture and robust coloring" were his exact words) but can't handle any athletic apparatus: balls, rackets, bats, you name it. Antoinette is an endomorph, tall and skinny. She doesn't like P.E., either. But now, heaven forbid, it seemed as if she were changing.

"You'll like it, MacBeth. I *guarantee* it."

"No way," I said firmly, but inside I wanted to try. Karate sounded so *exotic*, so *dramatic*. "When can you come over?"

"Tomorrow. Grandma May is coming over tonight to hear about our summer. I have to stick around."

"Okay. I'll be here."

"Great! See you!"

I hung up and plodded down the stairs to the kitchen. Friday night, and the same old thing. Set the table, eat, clear the table, wash the dishes, watch TV, and read. I had already checked *TV Guide*, and there were no good movies; nothing but dumb reruns.

Well, at least school starts in four more days, I thought in an effort to comfort myself. I usually like my teachers and I get good grades. Now if I could just insert some adventure and *romance* . . .

Mom had baked a healthful, but extremely dry, salmon loaf for dinner. She is trying to cook only low fat, low sugar, high fiber, high protein foods for us, since Dad is trying to lose weight, and, as she says, "Americans poison themselves with their diets!"

Fortunately, she hasn't outlawed sweets entirely, but life at our house is definitely whole wheat and natural. So I wasn't the only one who was shocked at Mom's announcement.

"Guess what? We're having Dash Honeycutt for dessert," she said.

My face flushed and my heart hammered in my chest. "Dash Honeycutt!" I cried. *"You're kidding!"*

"In one hour," answered my mother, calmly, and she got up to check something in the oven, something that was beginning to smell divine, like warm cinnamon.

"Mother! I don't believe it! *Dash Honeycutt!"*

"So what's a honeycut?" my ten-year-old sister Katie asked. "What's in it?" Katie is working on her foods badge in Girl Scouts. This week she has commented nightly on the exact number of dead insects the Food and Drug Administration allows in various foods. The mushrooms in tonight's dinner, she had reported earlier, had twenty maggots per 100 grams.

"If it's a honeycut, I hope it has lots of honey." That was Dad.

"It's not an *it*, it's a *he*," I explained. "Dash Honeycutt is an actor." I knew this because Mom and I had just seen his closing performance at the North Seattle Community Theater. Even from a distance, I could tell that Dash was dark, deep, and intense. Just my type. I imagined him to be just the type whose life was so packed with excitement that mere acquaintance with him would turn my life around.

When I had told Mom that I'd love to meet Dash, she said that she knew him personally, but I didn't believe her. I had read in the program that he had just moved to Seattle from San Francisco.

"Oh, preserve us all," Dad groaned. "She's bringing home another one from the theater."

Mom shook her head and made a face at Dad.

Dad excused himself to the study. "I need a few moments to collect my thoughts before the thespian arrives," he said and left.

"Are we eating a *man* for dessert?" Katie asked, giggling. "The FDA doesn't allow that!"

Mom laughed and slid an apple pie out of the oven. "No, a man is going to help us eat this for dessert!" She glanced at me and added, "He'll be here in forty-five minutes, plenty of time for you and Katie to clean up the kitchen."

Typical, I thought. Excitement, intrigue, and maybe even romance will be here in less than an hour, and life goes on as usual in the utterly average Langley household.

"Don't look so upset, MacBeth," Mom said. "I bet you'll even have time to finish a chapter of your mystery before Dash arrives." I threw the dishcloth at her as she ran out of the kitchen.

Probably the reason that my life is so blah is because

of my family. Even though my parents have interesting qualities, ours is still a mundane, suburban existence.

Dad designs people's yards. He is a landscape architect. The newspaper, specifically the *Seattle Times*, called my father "innovative and artistic, a master with indigenous foliage." He has dark brown hair, a large mustache, and soulful eyes. It's hard to tell if your own father is handsome, but I'd say Dad is pretty okay-looking. His only flaw is a slightly round belly, and, as I've said, he's working on that. If I were a play director, which is what I hope to be some day, I would cast my father as Sheriff Taylor of Mayberry, an Andy Griffith type: low-key and corny, but smart.

Mom has chin-length brown hair parted on the side, and she doesn't wear make-up. She's sort of a hippie, but she doesn't want to live in a log cabin or anything. She just wouldn't be caught dead in a three-piece suit. She was born rich and traveled throughout the world as a child. But as a young actress and playwright, she met my father and happily settled down to the life that I'm complaining about.

Katie always clears the table, and I load the dishwasher. Then I wash the pots, and Katie dries. The same old routine.

"What are you reading now?" Katie asked, shaking the placemats into the sink. Blond, freckled, easy-going and a fan of the Great Outdoors, she is the opposite of me. I have long auburn hair that I wear in a single braid and am into the even Greater Indoors.

"A book," I grumped. I didn't want to talk. I wanted

to think about Dash's arrival, what I would say, what I would wear.

"I bet it's a *sex* book." Katies grinned.

"Honestly, Katie. Is that all you ever think about?"

"Not all, but mostly." She giggled. "I think about rock stars, too." She handed me a stack of plates to arrange in the dishwasher.

Mom and Dad are spending a fortune sending Katie to Immaculate Heart parochial school, I thought. And here she is, a mere pubert, an undeveloped little twerp, lusting after boys and rock stars.

"You are a pubert," I reminded her. "And tomorrow is the last Saturday of summer vacation. You should be selling lemonade and playing kickball and reading Nancy Drew."

"I do that stuff, too," Katie explained, "when I need money or feel hyper or want a good book. Hey, did you see my new poster of Vile Kyle and the Vamps?"

"Are they the ones who all changed their names to 'V' names?" I asked.

"Yeah. Vile Kyle, Vixen, Vice, and Virgin."

"Virgin?" I said, amazed. "I don't believe it."

"Me neither." Katie laughed. "Hey, do you think you'll get a boyfriend this year? I want an older sister with a boyfriend. Laurie's sister is dating a guy, and Laurie watches them make out in his car."

I made a face. Laurie Lottman is Katie's best friend from Immaculate. Laurie's sister, Lucy, is my age, fifteen, and went from kindegarten through eighth grade at Immaculate with Antoinette and me. But she lost control at Harry S Truman High School and is now known as Loose Lucy.

My main source of information about Lucy is through Katie and Laurie. Lucy and I don't exactly operate in the same circles. Her mother, Mrs. Lottman, is a psychologist and is trying to get Lucy to like herself, which, in my opinion, is clearly not the problem.

"Don't hold your breath," I said lightly. "Every boy at Truman is immature and a dork."

"Ferguson isn't a dork."

"Ferguson Parrish has also been our next-door neighbor since we were in nursery school. He's like a brother. I want a guy to launch me into the spheres . . ." I caught myself before I spilled my guts. "Never mind."

"The spheres, huh?" Katie said and put away the last pan. "You're weird, MacBeth." She shook her head and strutted out of the kitchen.

I wiped off the table and counter, and then glanced at the clock. Twenty minutes and Dash would be here! I raced up to my room to get dressed.

Two

I scanned my summer wardrobe. Faded tee shirts and jeans. Nothing really fetching. I ended up in one of my many black turtlenecks. It was a sultry evening, and I would probably burn up, but I look good in black turtlenecks. I started wearing them last year at Truman, and now they're sort of my trademark. Mine and Katharine Hepburn's, that is. Katharine Hepburn is my favorite actress.

I was as ready as I would ever be, and I still had ten minutes to kill. I thought about how I had sounded like an A-Number One, First Class snob when I was talking with Katie. Probably not *every* guy at Truman was immature, I decided. I mean, isn't that statistically impossible?

I opened the top drawer of my dresser and dug out my secret list, my description of the Most Perfect Boy. I had worked on it all summer.

THE PERFECT BOY FOR ME
1. Tall, dark hair, Paul Newman blue eyes, "knowing" smile.

2. Sophisticated sense of humor (no bathroom jokes).
3. Small rear end.
4. Musical—plays piano, violin, or cello.
5. Intellectual and deep.
6. Magical conversational qualities.
7. Launches me to heights of grand passion.

If I could find this boy, I predicted, my troubles would be over.

When the doorbell rang, I peeked around the corner of the upstairs hallway, sort of the way an actor might peek at the audience before going onstage. Mom answered the door.

"Well, hello, Ferguson! How are you this evening?"

"Just fine, Mrs. Langley." He produced a large measuring cup from behind his back. "Can I borrow two cups of flour? I'm baking brownies."

Why did Ferguson have to show up now? I thought. Just when Dash Honeycutt was about to arrive. Probably he was here for a free dessert.

That business about baking brownies is a lot of nonsense because Ferguson Parrish got a *C* in Sophomore Cooking last year, and I know for a fact that there isn't a cookbook in the Parrish household. His mother threw them all away when she got divorced, as a gesture of freedom, she said. She knows all her recipes by heart, anyway.

I snorted and thumped down the stairs. "Good evening, Ferguson. Don't let us keep you."

"Ah, the fair MacBeth," he greeted me. "A vision of loveliness."

I felt a twinge of remorse for my remark, but I still couldn't bring myself to comment on Ferguson's loveliness. Ferguson Parrish is tall and painfully skinny, with stuck-out ears that he can wiggle at will, thick glasses, and braces. He assures me that he will be devastatingly handsome when the braces are taken off.

I can easily picture Ferguson as the bumbling deputy in a Western, only instead of a holster with a gun, he sports a wide belt with a sheath for his calculator. Ferguson is the type who takes watches apart for fun and spends all his money on photography and computer equipment. He is definitely not a leading man, but, in all fairness, he is a good friend.

"You see," he continued, "Mom is showing a house tonight, and I am starving. I've eaten dinner, but we are completely out of anything sweet. I found a brownie recipe on the back of the Hershey's Cocoa box, and, after surveying the pantry, concluded that I have all the necessary ingredients except the flour. I guess I could substitute whole wheat flour, but I'm not positive . . ."

I suppose he would have rambled on indefinitely, explaining his sad story, if I hadn't snatched the cup from him and headed for the kitchen. "Here. Take a cup of flour, take the whole crock," I said meaningfully, and reached for the brown ceramic container. "I mean I know you are being resourceful and domestic, and that's very admirable. But I'm sort of *expecting* someone, so if

11

you don't mind . . ."

Ferguson smiled wryly. "Are you asking me to leave? Because if you are, feel free just to say 'Get lost, Ferguson, oldest and dearest buddy.' What are close friends for, if not to understand and forgive rudeness? Are you *ashamed* of me, MacBeth?"

What a worm he could be. I felt myself grinning back at him, in spite of what he had said.

"I am not ashamed of you," I explained. "We're having Dash Honeycutt for dessert!" I clutched the flour crock to my bosom.

"What's that?" Ferguson asked, settling down into one of the kitchen chairs like Papa Bear, ready for his porridge. "Does it have honey in it?"

I scowled at him. "It's not a *what*, it's a *he*! He's an actor!"

Ferguson was silent, but his face said, loud and clear, "Big deal."

"Dash Honeycutt is Excitement Incarnate," I explained.

Ferguson regarded me thoughtfully. "I am an extremely exciting person, too." He grinned.

"I don't call calculators and computers exciting."

"*Au contraire*, MacBeth. I'll admit that there's not much glamour in science, but there's lots of excitement."

The doorbell rang. Mom strolled into the entry hall, and I felt the flour crock slip from my sweaty fingers.

CRASH! The crock burst into a cloud of white powder, coating my jeans and my black turtleneck, as well as the kitchen floor. Ferguson was closer to the epicenter of the explosion, so his face and glasses were caked with the chalky dust.

"Ferguson!" I shouted. "Look what you've done!" I frantically slapped at my jeans and then started coughing as the particles floated into my lungs.

"*Me!*" Ferguson cried, taking off his glasses. He was quite white and, I knew, quite blind. "I didn't do anything!"

And then, through the flour fog, I saw him rise and approach me, his hands groping for my chest. "Here," he offered, "let me help you. You're covered with flour."

In utter horror, I dodged Ferguson, the walking mummy. "I can see that, Ferguson!" I yelled. I staggered out of the kitchen, brushing my chest and gagging. The walking dead remained behind.

Katie came pounding down the stairs, and Dad peered out of the den, his reading glasses askew on the end of his nose, and queried, "That wasn't the dessert I heard, was it?"

"No," I moaned, and surveyed my appearance in the hall mirror. I had definitely faded, thanks to Ferguson.

Mom laughed and opened the door.

And there Dash was. Practically *naked*. I mean, all I could see was tanned skin and dark, swirling hair. He lunged for my mother.

"Di, *darling!*" Dash declared. "What an absolute *thrill* to see you again, after all these years! It's been *forever!*"

Mom pried herself away from the bronze skin, and I got a better look at Dash. There was plenty to look at. A slinky maroon tank top stretched over his giant chest, and, daring to look down, I saw equally skimpy nylon tricot shorts. Farther down, I noticed shiny silver and maroon Nikes, no socks, and, to my surprise, another pair of feet! These wore white, high-top basketball sneakers connected to faded blue jeans, connected to a black tee shirt, connected to a much younger version of Dash, without the gold necklace and earring.

Our eyes met. The electricity crackling between us was sufficient, I hastily determined, to light up Seattle for a month.

Dash was too old and too obviously athletic for me, I thought to myself sadly. For a brief moment I was grateful that Mom hadn't told me about Dash's visit earlier. This way, I had only an hour to anticipate and fantasize. Somehow that softened the letdown of actually meeting him.

This younger guy, however, looked just right, a fantasizer's dream come true! He had a aloof attractiveness that fascinated me, and when his black eyes wandered from my sandals, over my powdered jeans and gray turtleneck, and up to my dusty lips, I melted. Who is this guy? I wondered. I was getting impatient for the introductions.

But Dash gripped Mom's shoulders and eyed her from arm's length. "You look positively *radiant*, Di! Do you work out?"

"No," Mom said, wiggling free. "I do most of my work here at home."

Dash burst into laughter. His teeth were very large and very white. "Still as whimsical as ever! Gosh, it's good to see you!"

"Let me introduce you to my family," Mom said after she shut the door behind the quiet one, the one who was making my heartbeat roar in my ears and my breathing irregular. "This is my husband, Carl Langley," she said. "He's a landscape architect."

Dash clasped Dad's extended hand and shook it vigorously. Dad's tummy jiggled. "You're one lucky fella," Dash assured Dad. "Di's a first class act." He laughed and looked back to Mom. "Hey, that's a good one! As one actor to another!"

The quiet one leaned against the door, giving his father, if Dash was his father, a look of bored tolerance. I swallowed deeply. How could I even begin to describe this gorgeous guy to Antoinette? I wondered.

"And this is Katie," Mom continued. "She's ten."

"I once loved a woman named Katie," Dash said, sighing. "Remember, Di?"

Mom grunted.

"Bittersweet. Our relationship was so bittersweet." Dash hung his head, and we all had a moment of silence for Bittersweet Katie. I wondered if Katie was dead, or what? I made a mental note to ask Mom about it later.

"MacBeth," Mom said, gesturing toward me. "This is MacBeth. She and I saw your final performance last weekend."

"Breathtaking," Dash said, ogling me. "She is an absolute *vision*, Di." He reached over and touched my face. The flour film and my sweat had mixed to form a dough-like paste on my nose and forehead, and I knew that my cheeks looked as if they'd just been pressed in a waffle iron: mottled and red. My dramatic gray-black turtleneck only contributed to the pressure-cooker effect.

Dash did a complete inventory. "Perfect cheekbones," he began, his voice all oily. I felt a cold drop of sweat trickle from my armpit into my bra. "Hazel eyes, broad forehead, broad shoulders," Dash continued.

"MacBeth is broad where she should be broad!" Ferguson blurted out.

Embarrassed is such a weak word. I felt sick with humiliation, but I thought I had just enough strength left to kill Ferguson, and then finish myself off.

I looked over at the quiet one. He rubbed his jaw and stared at me beneath heavy, dark eyebrows. I was sure that lust was written all over my face for him to read. I wanted to pull my turtleneck up and hide.

"MacBeth is lovely," Mom confirmed, and then, thankfully, diverted everyone's attention to Ferguson. "And this is her friend, Ferguson Parrish,"

Ferguson made a goofy smile and saluted directly at the mystery person. "I'm MacBeth's friend," he announced.

"Ferguson's our next-door neighbor," I interrupted quickly, and noticed for the first time that he had managed to wash his face and glasses before appearing.

It was quite obvious to me that everyone had been introduced except the man of my dreams, my dark, brooding soulmate still leaning against the door with his hands shoved into his pockets.

Mom noticed, too. "Well, now that you've met my family," she said, "who is this, Dash?"

I stood, breathless, waiting to be introduced to The Perfect Boy for Me.

Three

"Oh, yes!" Dash whirled around. "Blake is so terribly quiet, I hardly know he's around! This is my son, Blake Honeycutt!"

Mom smiled sympathetically at Blake. "Hello, Blake. It's nice to meet you. Now, please go sit down, and I'll get some coffee."

Blake. Blake. What an exquisitely *masculine* name. I watched as *Blake* nodded to my mother, peeled himself off the front door, and slowly strolled behind his father into the living room.

Dad and Mom lingered in the hall for a moment. Dad groaned and gave my mother his don't-leave-me-alone-with-this-jerk look.

"Perhaps you'd like to make the coffee, Carl?" Mom asked loudly.

"I'd be happy to, Diana."

"Thank you, Carl."

"You're welcome, Diana."

We drank our coffee, Katie and Ferguson preferring milk; and we ate our pie, Dash preferring mild Danish Havarti to ice cream, and Mom saying that the best she could do was Safeway cottage cheese. And we listened to Dash. He talked about himself and his past, his future, his aspirations, his perspirations.

I ate slowly and tried to look interested but was actually keenly aware of Blake. Blake had a perfect view of me, but I had to turn and took past Ferguson to look at him. It was excruciatingly awkward, and I was edgy because of the strain. I tried to concentrate on Dash's troubles with admirers at his spa.

But I began to imagine that Blake was staring at me, his brooding eyes glazed with passion. When I managed a quick peek at him, as I set my dessert plate on the coffee table, he seemed to avert his eyes quickly. Probably he was so shocked by the chemistry going on in his body that he had to look away.

Then, suddenly, I realized that I had sweat on my upper lip. Large beads of sweat. I couldn't swab my face with my shredded napkin, which has absorbed all the moisture it could from my palms and now lay limply next to my plate on the coffee table. The only alternative was to mop my pasty face with my sleeve. I decided it would be more refined to just lick at the droplets when Blake wasn't looking.

For most of the conversation, I was tense and self-conscious. By the time Dash stopped talking about himself and started talking about Blake and the new play Dash was acting in, I was exhausted.

"It's a fantastic script! A spoof of *Dracula*!" Dash enthused. "Blake's working on the play, too. He's a stage-hand, aren't you, Blake?"

"Yeah," Blake said, staring at his lap. I admired his soft-spoken, Man-of-Few-Words approach. He seemed so sincere, so sensitive, so *spiritual*.

"I believe," Ferguson said, grinning, "that there is an old saying that fits here. 'Behind every great actor is an even greater stagehand,' or something like that. Right, Blake?"

"The theater is okay," Blake said, "but I like basketball better."

I cringed slightly. Oh, well, so what if Blake was a jock? In any relationship there are sacrifices to be made, adjustments to each other's lifestyle. Surely Blake would see that.

"Hey, do you play basketball?" Blake asked Ferguson.

"Not if I can help it," Ferguson replied with a smile.

"*Basketball*," Dash scoffed. "That's all Blake ever thinks about." Then, to my mother he said, "It's about time our kids should be considering their careers, don't you agree? They have to start planning their futures."

Our future, I thought. Blake's and mine. Yes, we must start thinking about it, Dash. The sooner the better.

Mom shrugged. "There's no hurry," she said.

Dash shook his head. "I guess you don't need to worry, since you've got a gorgeous daughter, but I've got a son to worry about. A future breadwinner."

Mom looked like she was going to grab Dash's throat, but Dad saved the day. "Do you like to dish, Fash?" he asked. "Uh, I mean fish, Dash?"

Katie burst into a fit of giggles.

Dad cleared his throat. "The salmon are running now. Great time to get out on Puget Sound!"

Mom started laughing, too, and Dash's life was spared. Dad gave her his cool-it-if-you-can look. Dad has lots of looks.

Blake didn't respond to any of this. He shifted, and then looked in my direction.

I blinked.

Mom noticed my silence. "Dash's play sounds fascinating, doesn't it, MacBeth?" she said. "We will have to see it." I didn't respond.

"Tell me, Diana," Dash said, "are you working on another play?"

"Why, yes, Dash," Mom replied, very politely.

"May I ask what it is about?"

Mom grinned. "A Soviet double agent."

"Oh, that sounds *intriguing*. I'd love to read it. I'm always interested in new plays by ingenious, prize-winning playwrights." Mom has won several playwriting contests and had two plays produced off-Broadway.

"I'm sure you are," Mom said. Then she added, "MacBeth loves plays, don't you, MacBeth?"

Blink. Blink.

"MacBeth?"

Blink. Blush. Where were my cue cards? I couldn't remember how to talk.

Dash was looking at me strangely, with sort of a crooked grin. Then he glanced over at Blake and back to me.

"You should audition for *Dracula*," Dash finally suggested. "Blake didn't want to." He glared at Blake and then looked back at me. "Do you have any experience?"

I shook my head and thought about how grossly lacking I was in the experience department.

"Hey, that's okay! We can work with you on a small part." Mom looked at little startled. I was flabbergasted. Was this called Being Discovered, or what?

"I want to see *Dracula*!" Katie whined.

"Yes, you probably would like this one," Mom said to Katie. Then she turned to Blake. "When does the play open, Blake?" She was trying to draw Blake into the conversation, but, unfortunately, it wasn't working.

"It's not going to open at all," Dash interrupted, "unless we can find some technical help. There's lots of light work in this one."

"Ferguson could do it!" Katie announced proudly. "He takes pictures for the school newspaper and knows all about lighting, right, Ferguson?"

"Oh, Katie, I love you," Ferguson quipped. "You spot talent so quickly."

Katie giggled. "It's true!" She looked at Ferguson admiringly.

Blake looked at me, and I felt compelled to speak, if only to appear halfway lucid. "And he's cheap, too," I said.

Ferguson laughed. "What a fan club I've got here. And I've always been a sucker for a spoof, even if it is a spoof on a vampire. Tell me what you need done."

Apparently Dash deemed Ferguson worthy, since he just told him to show up Tuesday after school. Blake would be going to Truman, too, and he and Ferguson could come to the theater together. I envied Ferguson for the first time in my entire life. And that's when my plan first occurred to me.

Dash and Blake left. The final straw for Dad was when Dash kissed Mom right on the mouth, in gratitude for bringing him seconds. Dad announced that he was glad to have met them, but he had to meet a client early in the morning, and they'd have to do it again some time. Soon.

Blake shoved his hands in his pockets and left without gazing into my eyes one last time. Yet surely he knew that I was his soulmate, the one that he had been searching for.

Of course, I realized suddenly. That was the very reason he denied himself one final look. He didn't want to be too obvious.

Dad shut the door behind Dash. "I need a drink, Diana."

"I'll join you," Mom said.

"I need one, too," Katie said and giggled. "A good stiff drink of sugar-free raspberry Kool-Aid. And I'm still hungry, too." I guessed that she wanted another slice of pie.

Ferguson laughed. "You're worse than I am, Katie."

"You can have a peanut butter sandwich," Mom said.

Katie winced. "Peanut butter has thirty insect fragments per 100 grams," she said.

"Fragments?" Dad asked.

Mom made a face. "The flour is still on the kitchen floor, MacBeth," she said, wearily.

"I'll clean it up in a second," I promised, and glowered at Ferguson. I decided not to bring up the flour incident, though, since I needed his cooperation for my plan.

My family promenaded into the kitchen and I was left in the hall with Ferguson.

"I've got a favor to ask you, Ferguson." I checked to make sure Katie wasn't spying on us. She wasn't. "It's personal," I said.

Ferguson's brows lifted. "I'm interested," he said with a leer.

"Knock that off. This is purely business. I don't fool around."

"I understand." He tried to smother a smile.

"It involves your contact with Blake."

"I figured."

I hesitated since I didn't think my interest had been that obvious. But Ferguson knew me pretty well. I guess I shouldn't have been surprised.

"I'll be frank then," I began. "I'm very interested in Blake. And I need your help to get close to him. Maybe you could even set up something between us, now that you'll be working together."

Ferguson looked at me thoughtfully. "What exactly do you want me to do?"

"Not much," I answered. "Just mention my name to Blake and do whatever else seems appropriate to encourage him to ask me out on a date."

"Using whatever means I deem necessary," Ferguson paraphrased. "Hmmm, how about bribery and black mail?"

"Ferguson," I said evenly, "try telling him how so-phisticated I am." I brushed a smudge of flour from my shoulder.

Ferguson grinned. "For how long?"

"Until he asks me out, I guess."

"No offense, MacBeth, but what if the impossible happens, and he doesn't want to ask you out?"

I groaned. "Okay. Let's say until he asks me out or I call off the whole effort. I'm not going to turn into one of those boy-crazy girls who keeps hanging on to a lost cause," I lied.

Ferguson considered this for a moment, and then said, "I'll help you only if you agree to my terms."

"Naturally. And what exactly are your terms?"

"That you bake me something sweet and delicious whenever Blake contacts you. That is, after we deter-mine that it was my doing."

"Mom won't let me," I protested. "She doesn't want us eating lots of sweets." Actually, the real reason I objected was that this was a grossly male chauvinistic bribe.

"Just say it's for *me*," Ferguson countered.

"You're crazy, Ferguson." And then I thought of Blake, and his dark eyes, and how they seemed to be repressing passionate impulses. I knew Blake had felt the chemistry, too. It was so obvious. Even our black clothes matched.

"It's a deal," I said.

Ferguson smiled.

That night, in the privacy of my bedroom, I retrieved the secret list from my drawer and made some mental notations.

1. Tall, dark hair, Paul Newman blue eyes, "knowing smile"? Yes, yes, no, yes. But Blake's eyes are better than Paul's, any day.
2. Sophisticated sense of humor? Can't check until next week at school.
3. Small rear end? Definitely.
4. Musical? Seems unimportant now, but will check into.
5. Intellectual and deep? Probably.
6. Magical conversational qualities? Need to be alone with him to determine.
7. Launches me to heights of grand passion? AND *HOW*!

There were some gaps in my knowledge of Blake, I had to admit. But if Ferguson did his job correctly, those holes wouldn't be there for long. And I could always quiz Mom.

I imagined Antoinette's amazed expression tomorrow when I told her about Blake and how things were going to be different for MacBeth Langley this year at Harry High!

My hand shook with excitement as I replaced the list and crawled into bed. I always read before I go to sleep, so I reached over to my night stand and rummaged through the stack of mysteries that Katie thought were sex books. I picked out the little book with the green cover and white lettering that said *The Thirty-Six Dramatic Situations*.

Mom had given me the book as a gift for graduation from Immaculate. I flipped the book over and looked at the advertising blurb.

> Georges Polti rendered a valuable service to authors when he discovered and classified the thirty-six dramatic situations. Under the command of the writer, an infinite number of possible combinations is brought into play.

Hmmm.

Georges Polti might have written the book for writers, but I saw another, *better* use for it. If anyone yearned for dramatic situations in her life, it was me. If anyone longed for an infinite number of exciting combinations, it was me.

And this little book listed all the dramatic situations in the whole realm of human emotion. I figured that *The Thirty-Six Dramatic Situations* could be my guide as I discovered the new and exciting life that lay ahead of me with Blake!

Nervously, I flipped through the pages, and, after several moments of intense study, I found my first situation. There it was in bold black print:

Ninth Situation
DARING ENTERPRISE

The situation called for a clever plan, a bold attempt, and then victory. I scanned the subclasses and found my situation in subclass D(2)—*Adventure Undertaken for the Purpose of Obtaining a Beloved Woman.* I drew a small line through the "Wo" in "Woman," and closed the book with a sigh of satisfaction. Romance would be mine this year! I was determined.

Just then Katie knocked softly on my door and stuck her head inside. She saw me reading, so she made some grotesque kissing noises and said, "Have they done *it*, yet?" and then pattered down the hall to her room, giggling.

Four

"**A**ntoinette is coming over," I announced on Saturday morning. "*She* had a very exciting summer."

". . . guess I could have a Russian double agent try to strangle Dillman, but strangulations are disgusting on stage," my mother, the crazy playwright, was saying. She stood in front of the closed refrigerator, pressing her forehead against the freezer door. Dad sat at the kitchen table with Mom's script and a pile of naked pancakes in front of him.

"What kind of name is Dillman?" Dad asked, chuckling. "Does he look like a pickle?"

"Dillman becomes a spy for the Soviets, Carl," Mom said. She stood swayback and stuck her rear end out, her forehead still glued to the refrigerator. "But he keeps goofing up his assignments."

"Do they call him Dillmanov?" Dad joked.

I cleared my throat. "Antoinette is coming over," I repeated loudly. "She has returned from the Orient."

"Good morning, MacBeth!" Mom said cheerfully, and pried her forehead off the refrigerator. I could smell

29

decaffeinated coffee from the doorway. "You're up bright and early for a Saturday." I decided not to remind her that every day was the same during the summer, Saturday or not.

"What's with you and the refrigerator?" I asked.

"Couldn't you tell? We were communicating. A mind link." She laughed. "It's thanking me for allowing only healthy food in this house."

I cast a sideways glance at Dad. He saw me, and we both shook our heads.

"Healthy?" I grumbled. I pointed to the offensive coffee pot on the stove. Then I plodded over and, with thumb and index finger, removed the limp filter containing the grounds. "You call this healthy? It smells like something from the sewer." I plopped the dripping wad into the trash.

Mom shrugged, and I remembered the question I wanted to ask her. "What do you know about Blake?" I asked casually, hoping she wouldn't make a big deal of my asking.

"Nothing."

So much for making a big deal out of it, I thought. "*Nothing?*" I repeated.

"Nothing. Zero. Zilch." She dropped into the chair next to Dad. "I didn't even know he existed before last night."

"What about Dash?" I asked. "What is he *really* like?" Even though I'd seen plenty last night, I thought a summary by Mom would be useful. At least she'd be talking about Blake's family.

Dad groaned. "Please, not while I'm trying to eat."

"To tell you the truth, MacBeth," Mom said, tilting her chair back on two legs, "Dash was, and probably still is, a womanizer, a cad, and a . . . *drip*."

I was incredulous. "Why did you invite him over if he's such a drip?" I asked sarcastically.

"Because you wanted to meet him."

That was true, and for a moment that seemed to be the end of the conversation. Then I remembered something. "What happened to Bittersweet Katie, the woman Dash remembered when he met our Katie?"

"She was one of the many whom Dash used and then tossed aside. Eventually she got over him. Now she works in an asparagus canning factory somewhere in the South."

"Good grief," I moaned. I felt so sorry for Bittersweet Katie. "Blake's not like that," I assured her.

"I don't know how you can be so sure," Mom said. "He was so quiet. He hardly said two words all evening."

"Still waters run deep," I quipped.

Dad laughed. "And deep waters don't drip, right?"

"*Dad!*"

Katie appeared in the kitchen doorway. "Are you talking about Blake?" she asked, but she knew we were so she didn't wait for a response. "Isn't he *darling*? Don't you think he's darling, MacBeth? I think he looks like Vile Kyle."

"*He does not!*" I cried. And then I cleared my throat and regained my composure. If anyone would make a big deal out of Blake, it was Katie. "Antoinette will be here at ten," I said, calmly.

"It'll be nice to see her again." Mom stretched and started gathering her papers together on the table. "I'd better get back to work. Be sure to stop by the study when she arrives, okay? I'd like to welcome her back to Dullsville." She smiled.

"I'm not laughing," I said, pointing to my scowling face.

"I noticed," Mom said.

Dad wasn't eating his pancakes. "I can't swallow these things without syrup to make them slide down. It's a physical impossibility."

I could see his point. "What about fruit?" I suggested. "Slice a banana over them, or something."

Dad looked as if I'd suggested he eat the coffee grounds. "No thanks," he said. Katie watched him closely as he gulped the last of his juice.

"Orange juice has one maggot per 250 milligrams," she reported.

Dad winced, and Katie amended her observation. "And that's not counting mites, aphids, thrips, or scale insects!"

"That's enough, Kathryn Elaine," Dad said sternly. "From this moment on, there will be no more accounts of the creatures in our food. Understood?"

"Understood." Katie grinned. "I'm finished with that part of my badge, anyway. Now I've got to prepare a complete cheap meal for my family. With all four food groups. The cheaper the better. The cheapest meal in the troop wins!"

"Cheap?" I said.

"You sound like a sick chicken, MacBeth!" Katie

cried. "Cheep, cheep, cheepcheepcheepcheepcheep-cheepcheep! Oooo! Say that word tons of times like that, fast. It starts to sound so funny!"

"I used to play that game when I was a kid," Dad said, perking up. "Try it with *pickle*. Pickle, pickle, pickle, pickle, pickle, picklepicklepickle, pic-cho, pi-co, p-co." He made a face, sucking in his cheeks and crossing his eyes.

"*Orange!*" Mom cried. "Orange, orange, orange, orange, orangeorangeorangeorange, oringe, oringe, joringe, jor-inge." She roared with laughter. "I can't even remember how to say it right!"

I couldn't believe this. "You're all crazy," I said. "I'm getting out of this loony bin."

"*Crazy!*" I heard Katie shriek as I climbed the stairs. "Crazy, crazy, crazy, crazycrazycrazycrazy ca-zee, cahzee—!"

Back in my room, waiting for Antoinette to arrive, I began to think about Blake and how my life would change when we were together.

First would come my popularity at school when everyone saw that Blake and I were a couple. Not that I care what people at boring Truman High School think. I *want* to be different, dramatically different. But the attention, I had to admit, would be nice.

After graduation, and after our wedding. Blake would work on Broadway and probably be discovered as a great actor! (After he got the basketball out of his system, of course.) He would be touted as the best young actor since Richard Chamberlain. I would go to every

Broadway performance, and Blake would wink at me from the stage. A knowing wink that we would share, and that would launch me to the moon!

After graduation, and after our wedding. Blake would work on Broadway and probably be discovered as a great actor! (After he got the basketball out of his system, of course.) He would be touted as the best young actor since Richard Chamberlain. I would go to every Broadway performance, and Blake would wink at me from the stage. A knowing wink that we would share, and that would launch me to the moon!

On "Good Morning, America" we would sit on the couch next to the host, and Blake would explain to the world about how I was the inspiration for all his love scenes. And then we would announce that we were going to Europe on tour!

Blake would act in London, Rome, Paris, and Madrid. It would be a full year's sweep: autumn in London, playing polo with Prince Charles; winter in the Alps, skiing and learning to yodel; spring, of course, in Paris, falling in love again at a little street café while nibbling croissants; and summer in Madrid, getting a great tan and taking matador lessons. We would refuse to kill the bull and get a special award from the Humane Society when we returned, in triumph, to the United States.

It was all so dramatic, so energetic, and it was all possible with Blake. Blake and MacBeth, forever.

When the doorbell rang, forty-five minutes later, I ran downstairs to answer it. Dad, I knew, had gone to a client's house, Katie was at Laurie's, and Mom was in her office, plotting the demise of Dillmanov.

Antoinette really had cut her hair. "Hi, MacBeth!" she cried.

"Hi. Your hair is *short*!" I was in shock. Antoinette's waist-length black hair was now mere stubble on the top of her head. Mere stubble, that is, that on Antoinette looked very cute and chic.

"I told you I cut it!" She bounded through the front door and dropped a tan gym bag on the floor. I cringed. Even the commercial aspects of sports, such as sweatbands, jogging suits, and gym bags, make me shudder.

"You're brave to chop it *all* off," I said. "I could never do that."

"Sure you could! Hey, I'll go with you! You can get yours cut before school starts."

"I don't think so." I wanted to be daring, but I wasn't ready for punk.

"Okay, but you'd look fantastic." Antoinette picked up the gym bag. "Come on. Let's go up to your room. You're going to love your present!"

"We've got to stop by the study first," I said. "Mom wants to welcome you back to Dullsville."

Antoinette laughed. "Your mom's so nice."

I wasn't surprised that Mom loved Antoinette's hair. She made Antoinette turn around several times, admiring it. Antoinette asked her about her new play, which Mom said she had just decided to call *The Decline of Dillman Glump*, and the two of them giggled like Katie and her friend Laurie Lottman. Finally I dragged Antoinette out of the study.

"See you later, Mrs. Langley," Antoinette said.

"Glad you're back," Mom said.

On the way up to my room, Antoinette sighed and said, "Your mom is so interesting. All my mom ever does is plan trips and go shopping."

"Interesting! *Please*, Antoinette, you haven't lived here all summer. Shopping and traveling sound great to me!" Antoinette shrugged.

In my room, with the door closed, Antoinette opened the tan bag. She pulled out a picture of a Japanese boy, decked out in a karate outfit: baggy white pants, long-sleeved white shirt, and a brown belt cinching it all together.

"Here is Yoshi," Antoinette said, giggling. I saw a glimmer of the old Antoinette, the pal who buried her Immaculate uniform beside mine in my mother's compost pile. The buddy who worried with me over all the horrors that awaited us at Truman, including co-ed P.E. classes.

"What's he wearing?"

"A karate *Gi*. Mine's in the bag, and so is yours!" She yanked two white pajama suits out of the bag and laid them on the bed.

"Mine?" I peeped.

"Yes! That's your present. Try it on!"

"It won't fit."

"MacBeth, quit being such a poop."

"Antoinette. How can you say that? Have you completely forgotten my vow to shun all forms of sport?"

36

"Karate is an *art*, MacBeth. Now don't give me any more trouble and put on your *Gi*. This is going to be fun."

I had to laugh. "Right, Boss."

"I'm your *Senpai*," Antoinette explained in a solemn voice as she undressed and slipped into the white uniform. "That means I'm a higher belt than you are. Any higher belt can teach a lower belt. Now take off your shoes. That's a sign of respect for each other."

I grunted. The *Gi* felt stiff and bulky. Antoinette tied a white cloth around my waist and a green one around her own.

"Now we'll kneel and fix our eyes straight ahead, as though to gaze upon a distant mountain."

I gazed at my poster that said "I rather be reading."

"Now stand up and we'll bow to each other, but keep looking at me. Always maintain eye contact with your opponent."

"Opponent? I hate fighting, Antoinette. You know that."

"Think of this as *self-defense*, MacBeth. What if a rapist or murderer attacks you? What are you going to do then? We have to be prepared for these things, you know. And with karate, you don't have to mortally wound the attacker."

"You've thought of every argument, haven't you?" I said, grinning.

"Yes. So do what I do. And don't be startled when I yell. It's mainly to empty my lungs, so I can breathe deeply, but it's also scary to the attacker."

"Right. Scary." Antoinette was really serious about this.

"Step forward, line your heels up, back foot at a ninety degree angle, front foot straight ahead, and bend your front leg. That's *zenkutsu dachi*, or front stance."

Antoinette made me bend my leg more. "Look, I could knock you over, easy," she said, pushing me.

"Okay, okay."

"*Aaaaa!*" Antoinette shrieked, and put an arm up over her forehead.

"Aaaaa," I repeated.

"Come on, MacBeth. From your *gut*." She slapped at her tummy. "*Aaaaa!*" she cried.

"*Aaaaa!*"

"*Aaaaa!*" Antoinette yelled again, and punched at the air.

I punched.

"Keep your wrist straight. A bent wrist can break."

"*Aaaaa!*" I called and punched.

"Alll riiight, Macbeth. You're a natural."

"*AAAAA!*" I cried. Block, punch. Block, punch, punch. This wasn't so hard, I thought.

"Now for a simple kick," said my *Senpai*. "Hold that pillow in front of your chest."

"Huh?"

Antoinette handed me my pillow and proceeded to show me the *maegeri*: her hands up in defensive position, karate stance, and then rearing back and snapping her foot out from her knee. SMACK! Right into the pillow she kicked. "*Aaaaa!*"

"*Aaaaa!*" I repeated.

38

"You're not supposed to yell if you're holding the pillow," my *Senpai* corrected.

"Sorry," I said.

"Just say, *Oss*. That means 'okay.'"

"*Oss*."

"Now you try. Remember to keep your back leg back, or you can be knocked over. Center of gravity is very important."

"*Oss*."

I was actually quite excited to try this kick. It was so dramatic, and highly impressive. Antoinette held the pillow to her bosom and I assumed the stance. I stared at that pillow, my opponent, a potential rapist or murderer. Block to the forehead. "Aaaaa!" Punch. "*Aaaaa!*" And then, leaning back, left knee up, and *kick*!

"AARRGGGG!" I missed the pillow completely and fell backward, crashing onto the floor and smacking my hand on the dresser. "Owwwww!" I cried.

Mom came running up the stairs and flung open my bedroom door. "MacBeth! What in the world? Are you okay?"

I cradled my throbbing hand and struggled to my feet, humiliated. "*Oss*," I muttered. Blessedly, Mom left without further comment, and Antoinette was very apologetic. She told me again that I was a natural.

"Look, MacBeth," Antoinette said cheerfully, "you only screwed up *once*. That's great! You should have seen me the first time."

"Okay, okay," I said. "I am good. But this isn't for me. It's not my style."

"So what's your style?" asked Antoinette.

What a perfect intro for me to tell her about Blake! Blake Honeycutt was my style!

"Oh, Antoinette," I began, "you won't believe this guy I met . . ."

Antoinette listened patiently. I even told her about the degrading deal I'd made with Ferguson.

"So why don't you audition?" she asked. "You'd be able to work with Blake, side by side!"

I shook my head. "What if I weren't any good? What then? I'd humiliate myself, and Blake would never get to see what a warm and loving person I am. No, I'll see him at school. Ferguson will be my contact at the theater."

Antoinette laughed. "*Contact*? You've been reading too many spy novels."

"Well, not anymore," I said. "Now I plan to *live* one!"

Five

First days of school are like opening nights in the theater. At least they seem like the way my mother describes the Opening Night Jitters. The worst part is the waiting; once the show starts, it's fun.

I got up, showered, made my bed, and dressed in the first-day-of-school outfit I'd carefully chosen the night before: rose-colored corduroys, black leotard top, and my quilted mandarin jacket.

Then I opened my window. It was a gray Seattle morning, and it smelled dewy and familiar. I like the rain and the coolness it brings, cleaning the world and awakening all kinds of natural smells. I could see a tiny corner of Green Lake. The water was still and silver, and I thought of Blake. He is a junior, so we wouldn't have any classes together, but lunch, maybe? I prayed that Ferguson would have at least one class with him.

By lunchtime I hadn't even seen Blake. How was he ever going to recognize me as his One and Only if he never saw me?

I was trying desperately to watch all entrances to the cafeteria, hoping that Blake would have the same lunch period I do, when a stack of school books dropped onto the table beside me.

"He's got second lunch," Ferguson announced. "So quit straining your eyes."

"How do you know?"

"He's in my English class, second period. He showed me his schedule."

I sagged over my peanut butter and reduced-sugar jam sandwich.

"But don't despair." Ferguson bit into a berry fruit pie, and then mumbled, "He asked about you."

I sat bolt upright. "*What*! He asked about me? What did he say?"

Ferguson's mouth was full, and I was about ready to strangle him as he chewed and slowly swallowed, his Adam's apple bobbing in his throat. "*What did he say?*"

"What did *who* say?" Antoinette sat down across the table from us.

"Hey, I like your new 'do,' Antoinette." Ferguson stopped chewing. "Reminds me of Liza Minnelli." He popped his eyebrows up and down. "Lots of razzle-dazzle."

"Hi, Antoinette," I said. "What did Blake say, Ferguson?"

"He just asked if you were going to audition."

"Then what did *you* say?"

"My exact words were . . . are you ready for this, MacBeth? Got a pen handy?"

"It's okay," Antoinette said, smiling. "I figured it out. You're talking about Blake." She bit into some gooey white stuff that looked as though it would be cheese when it grew up, but wasn't quite there yet.

"Antoinette, I'll talk to you in a minute, okay?" I flashed her a smile.

"What are you eating?" Ferguson asked Antoinette.

"Never mind what Antoinette's eating, Ferguson," I said, growing a little impatient. "If you don't tell me *this instant* what you said to Blake, I'm going to lay waste your body."

Ferguson grinned. "Oooo, that sounds like fun."

"*Ferguson*! We have a deal, remember?"

"Yeah," Antoinette chimed in. "You have a deal." She giggled.

"Okay, okay," he said. "I said, 'I don't know.'"

I waited for the rest, but there was nothing else forthcoming. Ferguson just bit into his sandwich.

"That's *it*? That's all you said? Blake asked you if I was auditioning, and all you said was 'I don't know'?"

Ferguson chewed thoughtfully. "No, I told him I'd meet him at the theater later because I have an orthodontist appointment at two-thirty."

"Your heart isn't in this project, Ferguson," I accused.

"What did you want me to say? You never told me if you were auditioning. And it just didn't seem natural at the time to comment upon your beauty and intelligence."

I hung my head and studied the marbled gray Formica of the cafeteria table. I really didn't know what Ferguson should have said, but what he did say seemed

43

woefully inadequate.

When I looked up, I surprised even myself with my determined tone. "Blake and I are going to get together despite you, Ferguson. We were made for each other."

Antoinette and Ferguson looked at each other, and Ferguson shrugged.

"Would anybody like a bite of my sandwich?" Antoinette asked. "It's delicious."

"I can see that," Ferguson said, making a hideous face. Then he crunched his lunch sack into a tight ball. "I've got to take a picture of the new science teacher for the paper. See you guys later." He trotted away eating a banana.

"What do you think about a karate club here at Truman?" Antoinette asked.

"What's to think?" I asked.

"Would you join it? You were really good on Saturday."

"Absolutely not," I said graciously. "I could get hurt."

Antoinette scowled and the bell rang. She popped the last bite of her pasty-white lunch into her mouth.

"What *is* that stuff you're eating?" I asked.

"Tofu. It's really good for you, and it's cheap. It's made out of soybean curds."

"Sounds yummy," I joked, and followed Antoinette to the cafeteria door. I hoped that Katie had never heard of the economical tofu.

"Hey, look." Antoinette pointed to a poster taped to the cafeteria wall.

"Looks like they're trying to pep up the newspaper this year," Antoinette said.

"Yeah," I agreed. "A personals column seems like a strange way to do it, though."

Antoinette continued to study the poster. "I just thought of something," she said, grinning. Antoinette had definitely changed over the summer. Last year her smile would have been called mischievous or playful, but the smile she was giving me now was nothing short of scandalous.

I looked back at the poster. "What?"

"I'll tell you this afternoon. I've got karate, and then I'll come over."

When the final bell rang three hours later, I was convinced that Blake Honeycutt didn't really go to Harry High, after all. I hadn't even had a glimpse of him and I couldn't understand it. Blake wasn't just another crayon in the box. He would never blend into a crowd. So where had he been all day? I was frustrated and depressed.

Antoinette arrived at four-thirty, punching and kicking her way into my room. When she set the gym bag down on my bedroom floor, I noticed that it made a heavy, metallic THUNK.

"What's in the bag this time?" I asked.

"Weights. I thought I'd get in a little lifting while we talked."

"Weights?"

"I'm really weak, MacBeth, and lifting is the best way to build muscle tissue. Everybody in my karate class lifts. Stomach work is the most important."

I groaned. "You've gone too far, Antoinette. I think I can safely classify you as a fanatic."

She laughed, and I watched lazily as she assembled the weights on my bed. "So what's your big idea?" I asked.

"The first dance is scheduled for September fifteenth, right?"

"If you say so."

"Well," Antoinette said in a giggly voice, "I'm going to advertise for a date!"

"*Advertise for a date*?" I was incredulous. "You've *got* to be kidding."

"I'm not! Look, you'll probably go to the dance with Blake, right?"

I blushed. Little did she know I'd already planned our honeymoon. "I hope," I said.

"So where does that leave me? Yoshi is three thousand miles of ocean away, and you and I went to the dances together last year, remember?"

I remembered. We talked the whole time, or danced

with Ferguson.

"I'm sure you don't want to take me on your date," Antoinette added, smiling.

I nodded vigorously, and we both laughed.

"Then will you help me?" she pleaded. "I can't think up good things to say, like you can."

"Thanks, but I'm not exactly experienced in this sort of writing."

"Nobody is. So let's just think up something silly, and anonymous, and see what happens, okay?"

"For you, anything." I said magnanimously.

Antoinette sat in my desk chair, a weight in each hand, lifting the weights to her shoulders and then straightening her elbows and letting her hands drop to her sides.

I sat on my bed, pen and paper in hand, writing down what the two of us composed. Antoinette insisted upon some terribly brazen parts, but I comforted myself by saying that it was anonymous, and that it was *her* ad, not mine. The following version is the one that we agreed would surely get Antoinette a satisfactory date for the dance:

> *Attractive female*, stable, intelligent, fun, seeks attractive, exciting male as date to dance, Friday, Sept. 15. Experience with women desirable, as well as a car, unlimited funds, and great dancing ability. If you have None of the Above, respond only if at least one of the above can be acquired by Sept. 15.

Put your name and phone number, addressed to Attractive Female, in the Personals Column box in Ms. Saglof's room.
Photos welcome.

"You're not actually going to put this in the paper, are
you?" I asked. I wasn't, I realized, up to Antoinette's
level of daring. Yet.

"Absolutely! This is going to be *fun*."

After Antoinette left, I sank onto my bed to brood
about not having seen Blake all day. Star-crossed lovers,
that's what we were. But our day would come. I would
make sure of it.

I reached for *The Thirty-Dix Dramatic Situations* to
find the name for this predicament. I knew that it
wasn't just coincidence that I opened the book right at
my problem. It was fate.

Twenty-Eighth Situation
OBSTACLES TO LOVE
(Two Lovers; An Obstacle)

How true! Never seeing one another was definitely an
obstacle.

I looked back at the book. Some of the horrible obstacles listed were: inequality of fortune and rank, like one
is a rich lord and the other is a peasant; previous com-
mitment to another lover; or relatives who won't let the
lovers get married, like in *Romeo and Juliet*.

None of these seemed possible for Blake and me,
thank heaven, although the very thought of them was

wonderfully dramatic. I especially like the idea of Blake, the exciting, handsome prince, falling in love with MacBeth, the poor, yet beautiful peasant girl who was trapped in drudgery.

Six

By Friday afternoon after school I was dangling at the end of my rope. My biology teacher had assigned us lab partners, and I got Jeep Hollingsworth.

Jeep had gone through Immaculate with Antoinette and me, so I knew him all too well. He is the Boys' Sports Editor on the *Bear Facts* now, and he thinks that this position makes him a handsome, strong athlete. In reality, he could win a Sesame Street lookalike contest for Bert, of the duo Bert and Ernie. No offense to Bert.

Another reason I was depressed was that after four days of school I still hadn't seen Blake. I was beginning to wonder if Blake was *avoiding* me. I was so despondent, I didn't even flinch when the telephone rang.

"Blake Honeycutt is on the phone," Mom said through my bedroom door. "Are you available to talk?"

I jumped off my bed and threw open the door. "MOTHER. *Of course I can talk!*"

"You can take in our bedroom."

"Thanks. Is it really Blake?" I whispered, following her out of my bedroom.

"That's what he said. But I suppose it could have been a fake voice. Maybe he's a Russian agent *incognito*. He's so dark and quiet." She laughed.

"Very funny," I said and scampered down the hall to Mom and Dad's bedroom. I lifted the receiver, tenderly put my hand over the mouthpiece and screamed, *"I've got it!"* I listened for the kitchen phone to be hung up, and then said, in a meek voice, "Hello?"

"Hi, MacBeth. This is Blake Honeycutt. Do you remember me?" It was Blake, all right. His voice was so low and alluring, I quivered. The electricity even went through phone lines.

"I remember you," I said shyly.

He paused, as if he expected me to continue, but I couldn't think of anything else to say. I just blinked.

"I've been looking for you at school," he finally said. "But I never see you. Have you been there?"

In that instant, I decided not to play games with Blake. Katharine Hepburn never played games. Anyway, the phone was safe. He couldn't see me sweat.

"I was there," I said. "And I looked for you, too."

Blake laughed. "Really?"

I sounded much too interested, I decided. I had to be more low-key. "Yeah. I thought we might have the same lunch, but I didn't see you." Not even Katharine Hepburn would let a guy know that she'd hunted for him all week.

"I've got second lunch," Blake said.

"I've got first lunch."

"Hey, are you sure you don't want to audition for Dad's play?"

I thought fast. Did this mean that Blake was interested in me? He must be. Why else would he call me to audition? He wanted to get to know me!

Ferguson had apparently said just the right thing, despite his lousy attitude. Blake had to contact me *himself* to find out.

The fact remained, however, that I had never acted before; I was scared I'd screw up my lines and humiliate myself. I'd always considered directing more my style. "I've never acted before," I explained. "I don't know if I'd be any good."

"I'm sure you'd be great, MacBeth." I could just see his dark, Omar Sharif eyes.

"I don't know . . ."

"Look, I'll help you, if you want."

I sucked in my breath. "You will?" I said in a You're-My-Hero voice.

"Sure. Look, I'll bring a script by tomorrow, to give you a chance to read the scene. Then, since Dad called off rehearsal for next Thursday, I'm free to . . . uh, practice with you. Is that okay?"

Was Seattle rainy? I couldn't believe this was happening. Was this really Blake on the phone?

"MacBeth? Are you there?"

"Yes! I mean, yes, I'm here, and *yes*, tomorrow and Thursday sound fine. Just fine." I was definitely babbling. Stop babbling, MacBeth, I screamed at myself. Get a grip.

"It will give us a chance to get to know each other better," he said softly.

"Uh, yeah," I cleared my throat. "I'd like that."

"I'll be over tomorrow at two o'clock with the script. Is that okay?"

"Two o'clock. Let me see. Yes, my calendar looks clear," I joked, and wiped my face. My *cheeks* were sweating. I didn't even know cheeks had sweat glands.

Blake laughed. "Hey, will your mom be around?" he asked.

"Huh?" I wasn't sure I heard him correctly. Did he ask about my mother?

"Your mom. Will she be there tomorrow?"

"Yeah, I think so," I said. What an odd question. But then I thought of the explanation. He didn't want to come over if an adult wasn't here, sort of as a chaperone. God, he was so classy.

"Okay. Bye."

I hung up and fell back on Mom and Dad's bed. I had a *date* with Blake Honeycutt!

Back in my room, I consulted my THE PERFECT BOY FOR ME list. Amazingly enough, I hadn't looked at it all week.

1. Tall, dark hair, "knowing smile"? Completely fulfilled.

2. Sophisticated sense of humor (no bathroom jokes)? Yes. Blake hadn't mentioned the bathroom once on the phone.

3. Small rear end? As far as I could remember, yes.

4. Musical? Actually, I had been foolish to make "musical" a requirement. What I had really meant was Mature and Disciplined. And the fact that he was willing to coach me so I

could read the scenes flawlessly, easily fulfilled the intention of Number 4.

5. Intellectual and deep? I would certainly be able to check this one off after Thursday, since Blake will probably tell me about his philosophy of *Dracula*, the whys and wherefores, as we read the script.
6. Magical conversational qualities? Yes, on the phone.
7. Launches me to heights, etc.? ABSOLUTELY!

Ferguson came over that evening. His TV was broken, he explained, and he wanted to watch a "Nova" special. I made a barfing imitation. But I agreed as long as I got to watch "Masterpiece Theatre" at ten. Then *he* made a barfing imitation.

I remembered that I had to talk with him, so I politely ushered him into the kitchen before the show started. He poured a glass of milk.

"Help yourself," I said.

"Thanks."

"Look, Ferguson, I've got news." I felt my heart start to race again, and I couldn't suppress my pent-up ecstasy. "I've got a date with Blake!" I cried.

Ferguson jumped, and some milk flew onto his shirt. "You don't have to scream," he complained, flustered, and looked down at his wet shirt. "I'm standing right here." He seemed overly upset for just a little spilt milk.

I dabbed at his shirt with the dishcloth. "I'm sorry," I said.

He pulled away. "When is the date?" he asked.

"He's coming over tomorrow! He's going to deliver the *Dracula* manuscript! And then he's going to read a scene with me next Thursday!"

Ferguson stood there, staring at me, as if he were trying to remember how to talk.

"I don't know whether I should audition or not, so Blake is going to *coach* me," I explained. And then, feeling generous, I added, "Under the circumstances, since you did help a little by being so vague in your response to Blake, I'll bake you something. But this is the end of our deal. I've got a date!"

Still no comment from Ferguson.

"The least you could say is 'Congratulations, Mac-Beth,' " I instructed.

"That's not a date, MacBeth."

"What? Of course it is! He's coming over here to see me. Just me. That means it is a date."

Ferguson shook his head. "Not really," he said. "A date implies *romantic interest*. Delivering manuscripts and reading scenes does not qualify."

I was incredulous. "Says who?"

"Says Webster, that's who. Let's look up 'date' in the dictionary."

"You are unbelievable, Ferguson. You're picking this thing apart, just to make me feel bad. You're a swindler who can't admit when he's wrong."

"Where's your dictionary?" he asked. I glowered at him and marched across the hall to Mom's study.

It galled me to admit it, but Ferguson had a point. I'm not one to argue for the sake of arguing, especially with someone like Ferguson. He is remarkably stubborn. The word "romantic" was not part of the definition of "date," but "social" was. It had to be a social appointment with one of the opposite sex. And, as I was forced to agree, reading scenes was not socializing. We were merely working together. This time, anyway.

So the deal was on. Ferguson would continue his efforts, and I was still seeking a bona fide date with Blake Honeycutt. Grudgingly, I remembered that I owed Ferguson the Creep a reward. Banana bread was all he would get out of me.

Ferguson penned the following definition, which both of us signed:

> A *date is a social appointment with a person of the opposite sex for the express purpose of love and romantic involvement.*
>
> Signed,
> Ferguson A. Parrish
> MacBeth J. Langley

On closer inspection, I didn't like the word "express" in there, as if a person had to announce the fact that he or she wanted romance. That could scare a person off. But I didn't have time to argue the point.

"MacBeth!" Katie called. "Where are you?" Ferguson and I stepped out of Mom's office.

"What were you two doing in there?" Katie asked, grinning.

"Good grief, it's just Ferguson," I said, embarrassed that she'd caught us together with the door closed.

How did the door get closed, anyway?

"Sure, sure," she said and giggled. "The show is starting, Ferguson."

"Right. Great. I've been waiting for this special all week. It's on theatrical lighting." And with that, he waved and followed Katie out of the study.

Feeling unusually warm and happy, despite the unpleasant episode with Ferguson, I sprawled on my bed to think about life. All of a sudden, it seemed, there were so many things to attend to.

I opened *The Thirty-Six Dramatic Situations*. I had checked off *two* Dramatic Situations in *eight days*. Already my life was starting to turn around, and I hadn't even gone out with Blake yet!

And now, Antoinette's ad was another dramatic experience. The advertisement was clearly the Twelfth Situation—OBTAINING. Georges Polti had a wonderful way of putting things. I giggled as I wondered what Antoinette would say if I told her that her ad was an *Effort to Obtain an Object by Ruse or Force*?

Now I had to concentrate on winning Blake Honeycutt's heart tomorrow. Attracting Blake, I knew, meant becoming sophisticated and exotic. But how?

Perhaps an accent would be appropriate. Yes, that's it. British would be nice, and I'd seen enough episodes of "Masterpiece Theatre" to know the formula for British. It was easy if you (a) stuck in "ayes," "says," "thens," and "mates" whenever possible, and (b) clipped off the ending sound of certain words.

"Say, you'd like anuther ale, then?" I asked myself in the mirror. "What's wi' all the gloom, eh mate? Mind, I'm not rushin' away just now, though, so's let's talk a bit."

Not bad, I thought. And extremely dramatic. I would start slipping bits of my new accent into conversation with Blake, sort of like the man on the Grecian Formula commercials who puts just a dab of formula on his hair each day, to slowly and inconspicuously get rid of the gray.

"Well, g'night, then, mate," I practiced again, softly, lest Katie happened to be passing. "I fancy 'tis time for my show."

"G'night, love," I imagined Blake answering.

Seven

"There's a big karate tournament tomorrow, MacBeth. Let me show you my moves before I go to the *Dojo*, okay?" Antoinette was standing on our porch clutching her gym bag. A white headband squeezed her head so tightly that her short black hair shot straight up.

"Sure," I said. "Come on in. Actually, I'm glad you're here. Blake will be here in five hours, and I'm about ready to lose what little control I still have."

Antoinette laughed. "Really? Blake called you?"

"He did indeed." I felt eyes looking at us and whirled around. Sure enough, the swinging door to the kitchen was slightly ajar, and I recognized Katie's eyeball. "Let's go upstairs, Antoinette, where we can have some *privacy*."

I followed Antoinette up to my room. "How come you didn't just wear your karate outfit?" I asked.

"It's called a *Gi*, and we're not supposed to wear it in public. It's in my bag."

"Oh." When we were in the sanctity of my bedroom, I locked the door and told Antoinette the entire incredible story. She was impressed.

"He really fell for you, MacBeth. I swear, it *must* have been chemistry."

"I've never felt anything like it before," I agreed. "Was it like that for you and Yoshi?"

"Not exactly," she said easily. "I wouldn't say that I *loved* Yoshi, but he was one of the most wonderful persons I've ever met. We only kissed once, when I was leaving."

What a romantic story, I thought. My heart was breaking for Antoinette and Yoshi, bidding each other farewell at the airport, kissing tenderly in the fog. It was Humphrey Bogart and Ingrid Bergman in *Casablanca* all over again.

But Antoinette didn't seem very depressed.

Obviously, I concluded, what I felt for Blake was far different from what Antoinette had felt for Yoshi. The power of my emotions, the sweat of my palms, told it all.

"Why don't you put your karate *Gi* on too, and I'll show you some new moves?" Antoinette pulled her *Gi* out of the bag.

"Uh, I don't know if it would be worth it," I stalled. "How long can you stay?"

"An hour. Come on, MacBeth. What will it hurt?"

Antoinette had just listened attentively to my Blake story. And since Yoshi was three thousand miles away, I figured I could unselfishly punch and kick at her in his place.

"Oh, all right," I grumbled. I snatched my *Gi* out of my bottom drawer.

"There's a class at the *Dojo* until ten-thirty," Antoinette explained.

"What in the world is a *Dojo*, anyway? It sounds like some extinct bird." I laughed.

"The karate gym, or school." Antoinette was not smiling. "It's got its own creed. Here, sit like I'm sitting."

Antoinette was on her knees with her right big toe over the left big toe, and her rear end resting on her feet. I checked to make sure the door was indeed locked and then copied the position.

"Now bow, like this." Antoinette leaned forward and placed both hands on my rug. I hesitated. "Do it," said my *Senpai*.

I bent forward, touching my nose to my hands.

"Put your butt down, MacBeth."

"I can't."

"Don't put your face down so far, then. And please, be positive. You *can* do it. You *can* do it," she chanted.

I stood up and bowed to my *Senpai*. "*Oss,*" I said.

Antoinette smiled. "*Oss.*"

For the next fifteen minutes, we did some warm-up stretches, worked on posture and focus, and reviewed the front stance.

"Now let's work on your punch," Antoinette said. "Remember your wind-up, then snap one hand back. The other punches out. Like this. *Aaaaa!*"

"*Aaaaa!*" I punched.

"Punch with your first two knuckles. *Aaaaa!*"

"*Oss. Aaaaaa!*"

61

"And relax a little, MacBeth. But pull your stomach and thighs tight. The tenser you are, the more tired you get, and your chances of winning are reduced."

Winning? Who did she think she was talking to? I felt like reminding my *Senpai* that I was a phony mesomorph, a non-athletic athlete, but I decided to maintain respect.

"Now for the kick again."

"Bleacch," I said.

Antoinette glared at me and picked up my pillow.

"Lower your stance. Squeeze your stomach. Maintain eye contact. Block to the forehead . . ."

The kick came back to me quickly. "Aaaaa!" I reared back, left knee up, and *smack*! A bull's eye.

"You're terrific, MacBeth! In fact, I'd say you're *gifted*."

"Really?" I asked, actually feeling good about that kick myself.

"Really! Please come to the tournament tomorrow," she begged and squeezed my shoulder. "You'd love it!"

I grinned and bobbed my head. "Okay!" I said in the fever of the moment. "I'll come!" Actually I had planned to read the *Dracula* script tomorrow, but what the heck. Antoinette was my best friend.

Antoinette changed into her street clothes and rushed off to the *Dojo*. I nestled down onto my bed and pulled out *The Thirty-Six Dramatic Situations*.

I had just experienced the Twenty-First Situation— SELF-SACRIFICE FOR KINDRED. This situation called for a hero (me), the kinsman (Antoinette—she was practically kin), and the thing sacrificed. I was sacri-

62

ficing the pleasure of reading Blake's and my scene, at least until Monday.

Blake was right on time. Mom was in her study and Katie was safely in her room. My heart bounced in time with Blake's basketball as he dribbled it up our sidewalk.

"Hi, MacBeth!" he said cheerfully, and he leaned against the side of our house. He held a folder under one arm.

I took a deep breath. "Hi." I couldn't exhale. I stood perfectly still.

"I'm going to shoot some hoops later. That's why I brought the ball." He bounced the ball a couple more times, and I admired his long, tanned arms. The veins in his forearms and hands bulged. His heart must really be cranking, I thought. Probably he was as excited to see me as I was to see him!

"Come in," I said. And then I remembered my accent. "How's it goin', then?"

"Okay." He smiled at me for a prolonged moment. "Actually, better than okay. Things are really looking up."

Because of me! I thought. He probably adores my accent.

"You've got beautiful hair, MacBeth," Blake said in his deepest voice. He touched my braid gently, and then let his hand rest on my shoulder.

I closed my eyes momentarily and felt his hand massaging my neck! My head was spinning. If his hand stayed on me much longer, I'd probably pass out.

"Is your mom here?" he whispered, letting go of me.

I nodded and blushed. "It's okay, Blake," I said softly. "She's in the study." He was such a gentleman. "Say, would you be likin' something to drink, then?" I asked.

"Sure," Blake said. His lips looked smooth and soft. "What have you got?"

Mentally, I scanned the refrigerator. "Milk, orange juice, iced tea, water, and sugar-free raspberry Kool-Aid."

"No Coke?"

"Nay. Mom doesn't believe in it," I explained. How could I expect someone like Blake to drink milk? I thought. I mean, *Ferguson* drank milk.

"Kool-Aid's fine. Thanks."

I ran to get the drink. When I returned, Blake was looking down the hall.

"Is that where your Mom works?" he asked.

"Yeah. Say, Blake, I really appreciate your doin' this for me." I sat on the edge of the couch.

"Like I said, it's my pleasure." He looked longingly at me as he sipped his Kool-Aid. "Your parents seem really nice," he said.

"They're okay. But your Dad is so much more interesting. I mean, he's an actor and everything." I couldn't seem to keep the accent up and concentrate on the conversation at the same time. Dropping in a little British every once in a while would have the same effect, I decided.

Blake shook his head. "My dad's a jerk. We don't get along at all."

"Really?" I said, accent forgotten. Who cared about being exotic during a heart-to-heart talk, anyway. Blake was baring his soul to me.

I couldn't help but remember Mom's assessment of Dash. Womanizer, cad, drip . . .

"He wants me to be an actor, like him, but I'm not interested," Blake continued. "I want to go back to California and live with my mom."

No! My heart screamed. *You can't leave without me!*

"Mr. James, my coach, had just put me on the varsity basketball team this year when my mom decided to get remarried. She's got two new stepkids now, and the condominium is really crowded. Dad insisted that it would be best for *me* to come with him to Seattle. *Ha.* Turns out it's best for *him.*"

I sat there, mouth agape. What did he mean, *best for Dash*? But I couldn't ponder Blake's semantics for long.

Part of me was thrilled that he was confiding his deepest feelings, but most of me was dying. Writhing in pain. I knew he'd feel a lot better about being in Seattle once our relationship kicked in. We just needed time together.

"Can't you play basketball here?" I suggested.

Blake shrugged and downed the last of his Kool-Aid. "Maybe. I don't know. I don't even know the coach."

"His name's Erlich," I said hastily. "I'll introduce you. *Tomorrow.*" Though how I'd find either of them on a Sunday was beyond me.

"You're nice, MacBeth." He stared at me. He looked completely absorbed. I shivered. "That's really nice of you."

I blushed. I'd do *anything* for you, I wanted to say. Don't you recognize me? Don't you see that spark flying between us? Please, don't leave me just when we're getting so close, when a lifetime of ecstacy is waiting right here for you at Harry High!

"Aye," I moaned softly.

Blake reached over, brushed some loose hair from my face, and rubbed my neck with his hand. I melted right into our Scotchguard corduroy couch.

"Mr. James was like a father to me," he explained. "A lot more than Dad ever was. All he cares about is himself. Do you understand that?"

"Understand . . ." I muttered deliriously.

"I'm glad." Blake pulled his hand away and I woke up out of my trance. "Here's the script," he said, and I thought I detected a bit of a blush in his cheek, too! "It's Act two, scene three. Hey, before I leave, would it be all right if I said 'hi' to your mom?"

"Mom?"

"Yeah." He smiled, and my mind went blurry again.

"Sure. This way." I knew he was concerned that Mom know he was honorable, but this would have made Sir Lancelot look like a bum.

He followed me to Mom's study.

"Hi, Mrs. Langley!"

Mom looked up, startled. "Well, hello, Blake. How nice to see you again." She gave me a puzzled look.

"I'm sorry to bother you, but I wanted to say 'hi' before I left."

"That's nice of you." Mom gave him her polite, I-want-to-get-back-to-work smile.

"Uh, is that your new play you're working on?"

"Yes, it is."

Blake leaned over to look at the paper in Mom's typewriter. "Act three, huh? I guess it's almost finished, then?"

Mom laughed. "Either it is going to be finished this week, or I'm going to be!"

Blake nodded. "You're a fast worker. Well, it was nice to see you again. And I'll see you on Thursday when I help MacBeth with her auditioning scene."

"Right," Mom said. "Thursday. Good-bye, Blake and MacBeth."

Only when I heard my name did I realize that I'd been holding my breath again. I let out a little sigh, and Blake reached for my hand and squeezed it gently.

"Bye, Mom," I whispered. My ears rang, and my windpipe was absolutely clogged with passion.

I walked Blake to the door and watched him dribble his basketball off into the sunset.

Eight

Sunday afternoon, before I left for Antoinette's tournament, Katie announced her dinner party. I found the invitation on my bed: formal dress; large appetite; at the Langley Happy Kitchen; Thursday evening, September 14, at six o'clock. Date required.

"*Why Thursday?*" I cried. "Blake is coming over on Thursday!"

Katie grinned. "Aunt Leah can't come on Friday or on the weekend."

"Aunt Leah is coming?" I groaned. Aunt Leah is my father's aunt, and undoubtedly the spaciest person I know.

"Yes, she is."

"And what does this mean?" I pointed to the "Date required" line on the pink and lavender invitation.

Katie looked puzzled. "What does what mean?"

"Katie, you know perfectly well what I'm referring to. Since when do invitations to dinner parties demand that a person have a date?"

"It's out of my hands, MacBeth." She opened her palms in a helpless gesture, and shrugged. "Mrs. Schweitzel, my

Scout leader, says that guests usually come escorted to formal dinner parties."

"Someone should welcome Mrs. Schweitzel to the twentieth century," I scoffed. "I'm quite capable of eating by myself."

"I have to turn in a guest list to Mrs. Schweitzel, and if it isn't *balanced*, then I probably won't win the prize."

I laughed shortly, "Ha! You said that the cheapest meal wins. You didn't say anything about balanced guest lists." We were standing in the kitchen arguing when Dad walked in and dropped a roll of landscape plans on the kitchen table.

"I'm asking Ferguson and Laurie to come together; Antoinette will be with Aunt Leah, but I'll write Leah's name on the guest list as Lee; Mom and Dad will be together, of course; you and Blake; and since I'm the hostess I don't have to have a date!"

"Don't mind me," Dad said. "Your mother is gone and I'm raiding the kitchen."

"Blake!" I cried. "You didn't . . ."

"He was more than happy to stay for dinner," Katie explained. "I asked him yesterday. I guess you were getting a drink, or something . . ."

"*You little . . . pubert!*" I was too furious to think. Instead I turned to Dad for help. "*Dad!*"

"What?" he mumbled, still opening and shutting the cabinets. "There is absolutely nothing I can recognize as food in this house," he said.

"Did you hear what Katie just said? Without asking me, she invited Blake Honeycutt to dinner!"

69

Dad looked nonplused. "Why would she have to ask you about that?" he asked, oblivious.

"Because . . . well, because . . ." I was trapped. Dad was right. Katie could invite whomever she wanted to her party. But how could I bear the humiliation of Blake coming over for a Girl Scout dinner?

"Yeah," the little hostess said smugly. "Why?"

"*Never mind,*" I growled through clenched teeth and marched out of the kitchen. I slammed my bedroom door and snatched up *The Thirty-Six Dramatic Situations.* My situation was easy to find. The Thirteenth Situation—HATRED OF KINSMEN. And I thought about her all afternoon and evening as I watched Antoinette and her friends punch, kick, and flip each other at the *Dojo.*

❋❋❋

I arrived at school on Monday morning, rested and primed for another day of hopeful searching. *I am going to casually run into Blake today if it kills me,* I told myself.

I had plotted a different route to each one of my classes, one that meant I had to navigate about two extra miles of hall in the same five-minute passing time, but eventually, I knew, I had to cross his patch. If only for the merest moment, as I sprinted down the hall, Blake and I would have contact. And the more contact, the better chance of his realizing that he had to stay in Seattle, to be near me!

I was not prepared to see Blake walk out of a Boys'

Restroom with Dean Boswell. I saw him, but he didn't see me. I stopped, frozen by the water fountain like one of those statues with water squirting out of its palms. He was with *Dean Boswell*. I turned and ran to my class without saying 'hi.'

All morning long, the picture of Dean Boswell huddling up to Blake plagued me. Dean doesn't blend into crowds either, but for a different reason. Half of his hair is bleached white and he wears a sleeveless jean jacket with a red skeleton painted on the back. He gives me the creeps.

I'd had only one encounter with Dean. It was the day before spring break last year and I was outside, waiting for Antoinette after school. Behind the gym, I saw a gang of hoods, Dean included. Dean was tucking a can of what looked like spray paint inside his coat. I say spray paint because the wall of the gym was covered with fresh graffiti, complete with crude illustrations. Most of it referred to the general subject of sex.

"Hey, get outta here!" he had shouted at me.

I was too startled to reply, or to move quickly enough for him, so he had swaggered up to me and grabbed my arm. "You saw nothing, right?" he had threatened. We were standing quite close together.

"Right," I had whimpered. Then I had edged by him and ran back into the school building.

I didn't look back, I was so scared, and Dean didn't follow. Slowly, as I walked home, the realization of what I had seen seeped into my brain. Then I was terrified. Nightmare kind of terrified. What if Dean got in trouble and thought *I* had reported him? Would I ever be safe at Truman again? Would I be yanked into the Boys' Restroom one day, only to have my body found, mangled and lifeless, in the school dumpster?

As it worked out, several other people had seen Dean and his vandals, and he was suspended. He doesn't even recognize me now, I don't think. I'm just another cowardly kid who he can intimidate.

So now I was worried for Blake. Dean could have had a knife to his back for all I knew.

I saw Antoinette briefly in the hall before lunch. "Hi," I said.

"Hi! I'm going to talk with Mr. Erlich. He said he'd sponsor a karate club if I wanted to start one!"

"Great." That reminded me that I needed to introduce Blake to Mr. Erlich, *soon*.

"Hey, did you see our ad in the paper?"

"*Your* ad," I said. "Yes, I saw it."

"Will you pick up the responses after school? I've got karate, but I'll come over tonight, and we can read them together, okay?"

"Sure, okay."

"Great!" Antoinette said. "Oh, and Katie left a message with my mother about her party! That should be *fun*!" And she ran down the hall.

Fun. There's that word again. I've got to have a serious talk with that girl about the definition of fun.

At lunch, Ferguson trotted across the cafeteria, waving a paper at me and grinning like he had just bought a new computer game. He dropped his books on the table, as usual. "Where's Antoinette?"

"Starting a karate club. Interested?"

"No way. I like my body in one piece, thank you." He laid the *Bear Facts* on the table and peered into his lunch sack. "I trust that the manuscript was delivered safely this weekend. Right?"

"It was," I replied, And then it occurred to me that I really didn't need Ferguson anymore. I knew now that Blake was truly interested in me. *Romantically*. He had held my hand, hadn't he? But, I reasoned, Ferguson could still be useful in convincing Blake to stay in Seattle. If Blake could get on the basketball team and meet some other guys, Dean would leave him alone.

"Ferguson?" I said in a very kindly manner.

"Uh-oh. I know that tone of voice. What can I do for you now, my dear MacBeth?"

"It has to do with Blake and our deal."

He gobbled a Twinkie. "I'm listening."

"Well, keep saying whatever you're saying to Blake. I think it's starting to work." It's smart, I've noticed, to compliment a person before making a request.

"Uh-huh," Ferguson said. "I do good work."

"But Blake misses his basketball team in San Francisco. Maybe you could introduce him to Mr. Erlich."

"Huh?"

73

"Blake doesn't get along with Dash, and he wants to go back to San Francisco. Mr. Erlich coaches basketball, and maybe Blake could get on the team."

"Oh, I get it." Ferguson bobbed his head. "Okay, but this additional work will require additional energy . . ."

"*Ferguson!*"

"You'll owe me another baked delight, MacBeth. And, please, skip the banana bread. No offense, but I ate one slice of that loaf you baked and said good riddance to it."

"Speaking of good riddance . . ." I stood up, glared at him, and marched away. Ferguson could be such a butt.

The rest of the day dragged. All I could think about was reading the manuscript Blake had given me and picking up those ad responses for Antoinette after school.

I wondered who the "attractive, exciting male" applicants would be? This was rather intriguing, I had to admit, even though I knew no guy could come close to Blake. It was still a very dramatic situation.

When I checked the box after school, I was delighted to see two notes addressed to Attractive Female. I suppressed my desire to rip them open. I'm a trustworthy friend, I reminded myself. I do not read other people's mail. I regard spying as a loathsome activity.

With that in mind, I only held the folded papers up to the window. Nothing. The letters were folded too many times. I bit my fist in frustration and shoved the two responses into my purse.

74

Nine

As I walked home alone past Green Lake, I watched the joggers and a couple of elderly dog-walkers enjoying these last bits of brightness before the rain would descend on Seattle for the winter. I wondered if Blake liked Green Lake, and if he'd like to go for a walk together, talking about our future? When I stopped by the grocery store for brownie fixings (for Ferguson, the butt), I wondered what Blake's favorite foods were.

"I'm home!" I cried when I walked in the door, loaded down with my groceries. Mom was standing in the kitchen, her back to me. "Hi!" I said. "How's it going?" I dumped my purse and books into the rocking chair.

Still Mom didn't turn around. She grabbed something off the counter next to her and crumpled it until it disappeared into her fist.

"Mom?" I asked, concerned. Her shoulders were haunched, as if she'd been crying. "Are you okay?"

"Mmmmm," came the muffled response.

"I'm going to bake," I said, and set my bag on the kitchen table.

"Mmmmm." Mom bent over, opened the cabinet under the sink, and deposited whatever was in her hand. Then she turned around, slowly, dabbing at the corners of her mouth.

"What were you eating?" I asked.

"Oh, nothing," said my mother. She remained planted in front of the cabinet. "Dash called and asked about my play," she said.

That's nice, I thought. I wasn't going to let her change the subject. Who cared about Dash, anyway?

"Nothing? What's *nothing*? Surely you remember what you just ate." I was beginning to have a sneaking suspicion of what she had just consumed.

"Of course I remember," Mom answered, and smiled guiltily. "What are you going to bake?"

Nice try, Mom, I thought. "Mother," I said, "I see the remains of something chocolatey-looking on your lips."

"Oh, don't be silly, MacBeth," Mom said, and picked self-consciously at what I thought were pieces of peanut between her teeth. "We've got some lovely apples if you want to bake an apple crisp."

"Really? There weren't any apples when I packed my lunch this morning. I looked all through the fridge." That, of course, was a lie.

"I bought a whole box last week," said Mom, puzzled. "I can't believe they're gone already." She moved toward the refrigerator and I lunged for the cabinet, flung open the door, and pulled out the trash can.

Yuk. Trash. Coffee filter, no. Milk carton, no. Empty tomato sauce can, no. But wait. A wad of brown paper was stuffed into the tomato can.

I retrieved and uncrumpled the increasingly familiar remains. A tomato-spattered Snickers wrapper.

"Well, Mom," I said. "What do you plead? Guilty as charged?"

"Guilty as charged," Mom said, embarrassed. "I couldn't resist it at the store today."

"Got any more?" I asked, smiling.

Mom nodded. "One." She skulked over to the junk drawer, the hiding place.

She and I split the candy bar. Then we both ran to the bathroom to brush the evidence out of our teeth.

Antoinette arrived just as I was sliding the brownie pan into the oven. Mom and Dad had gone out jogging, and Katie was in her room listening to Vile Kyle.

"How many?" she asked the second I opened the front door.

"Two."

"Alll riiight!" She pounded up the stairs in front of me. I displayed the two folded notes on my bed. "Which one should we read first?" she asked, smiling greedily, as if she were trying to decide between two pastries.

I pointed to the one nearest me. "This one."

Antoinette had a hard time opening the note; it was tightly folded into a triangle. Immature guys at school flick folded triangles like this one around on their desks, playing miniature football. I should have been suspicious, but I wasn't. Finally, Antoinette held it up for both of us to read.

Dear Attractive Female,
   You call yourself *stable*? I'd call you crazy. But I'm willing to give you a chance. I'm sure you'll know who I am, so I'm not enclosing a picture.
                                      Signed, Jeep Hollingsworth

"*Jeep Hollingsworth!*" we both cried in unison. Antoinette laughed. "Don't you *dare* tell him that I'm the Attractive Female!" Antoinette knew that Jeep was my biology lab partner.

I laughed, too. Antoinette Bigley-Barnes was no more Jeep Hollingworth's idea of a dream date than he was hers. "Never," I promised. "He would probably faint and crush some poor, unsuspecting bystander."

"At least there's one more note," Antoinette said, and opened the other letter. Again she held it up. Antoinette giggled as she read it.

Dear Attractive Female,
   Many call me cad, several have called me a rascal, and some say *scoundrel* the second they hear my name. Interested?
   I am the basketball type, a lean and mean machine, but I am also a sensitive, lonely soul. I need an enchantress like you in my life.
   If you're interested in the evening of a lifetime, seal your response, along with your name and phone number, in a plain white envelope addressed to *Scoundrel*,

and put it in the Personals Column box before school tomorrow morning.

"Isn't this *cute!*" she said when she was finished.

"It doesn't say if he has a car or unlimited funds or great dancing ability," I reminded her.

For some reason, the letter reminded me of Dean Boswell. Dean was smart enough to write this. But it puzzled me that he called himself the basketball type. That was more like Blake.

"That stuff doesn't matter," Antoinette said. "This guy sounds *interesting.*"

"Interesting? He calls himself a scoundrel! Do you want to go out with a scoundrel?"

"He also says that he is a sensitive, lonely soul, Mac-Beth." Her voice suggested that that should be the final word on the subject. After all, what more could a girl expect from a personal ad?

But I couldn't drop it. Antoinette could be in for Big Trouble if it was Dean, or someone like him. "Scoundrels always say they're sensitive, lonely souls," I warned. "It's part of the scam."

She stared at me. "MacBeth, do you know who wrote this?"

"How would I know that? I'm just cautious."

"I thought you were the one who wanted excitement and intrigue."

"I do. I just don't want you to get hurt."

Antoinette laughed. "Come on," she said, "help me write a response to this scoundrel. And, if it will make you happy, I won't tell him who I am, yet."

"Okay."

I wondered if there was a limit to Antoinette's daring. It occurred to me that writing anonymous letters was like talking on the phone. A person feels freer to be bold because the person on the other end is invisible. At least, that's my explanation for Antoinette's reply.

Dear Scoundrel,
    I'm interested. But I need more information before I will go out with you. Please answer the following questions:
1. Do you already have a girlfriend?
2. Who wrote *Sense and Sensibility*?
3. Have you ever killed anything other than insects?
4. Have you ever done the laundry?
5. Who do you think is the most beautiful woman in the world?

Put your answers, along with your name and phone number in an envelope addressed to *Enchantress*, and put it in the Personals Column box before school Thursday morning.

Antoinette had searched my bookshelf for something classic and had decided upon *Sense and Sensibility*. I told her that no boy at Harry High would know that Jane Austen wrote it.

"I don't agree," she had said. "Besides, the Scoundrel is the only one this concerns, and he can look it up. If he's still interested."

Now that the letter was finished, I reread it. "You are nuts," I said.

"I know, but I'm finding out more about him. Look." She held up her letter and pointed to each number.

"Number one tells me about Faithfulness," she began. "Number two, of course, is the Intelligence question. Number three is Sensitivity, four is Helpfulness, and five, well, five is five."

"Well," I said, resigned. "It looks as though *you're* going to have a date." I sighed. "I hope Blake asks me to the dance when he's here on Thursday."

"You *really* like that guy, don't you?

"Yeah. It's weird. We haven't talked a lot, I know, but I feel like I've known him all my life," I said. I just hoped Blake was still in one piece after his brief contact with Dean.

Antoinette looked dubious, so I changed the subject. "Hey, Antoinette, would you do me a favor?"

"Anything, you know that."

"Would you go shopping with me tomorrow? I want to buy some make-up and stuff for when Blake comes over."

Antoinette frowned. "Why? You don't need make-up. You're one of the prettiest girls at Truman."

"Yeah, well," I said, blushing, "I want to make sure that Blake sees that on Thursday. It's important to me, Antoinette."

"Okay, I'll go with you *if* you let me show you another karate move," she said.

I groaned. "*Antoinette.*"

"It's a simple throw."

"A flip?" I interpreted.

"Yes. All you have to do is get your opponent off balance, and then grab and twist . . ."

"*Oss*," I said, and bowed to my *Senpai*. I was better at my first throw than my first kick, but Antoinette offered no resistance. It was easy. She bounced off the bed, where I had just thrown her, and praised my ability.

When Antoinette left, she entrusted the ad to my care, since she didn't have any classes near Ms. Saglof's room. "You'll be sure to put it in the box tomorrow, right?"

"Absolutely," I said. "You can count on me." And then I bowed and said, "*Sayonara*."

She bowed to me, too. After karate training, Antoinette had explained, the student and the *Senpai* bow to one another, thanking each other for sharing time and knowledge. She was determined to make a convert out of me.

❋❋❋

In my room after dinner, I curled up on my bed with the *Dracula* script. Blake had touched this script, I thought happily, and held it against my heart.

Blake had said Act II, scene 3. I opened the folder and began reading. I read slower and slower, trying to absorb each horrifying line. I couldn't do what I had to do in the scene! I *just couldn't*. I didn't know *how* to do it, number one, and number two, I was too embarrassed.

Dracula comes into my bed in the middle of the night intending to bite my neck, I tell him to get lost, he insists, and then I kiss him, "passionately"!

This was ridiculous. There must be some mistake. No, there was no mistake. This was the work of that despicable Dash! Mom should have hung up on him this afternoon. Why did she say he had called? The jerk. Blake probably had no idea of the scene when he volunteered to help.

And now — I thought about the kiss again — I couldn't back out of the audition. If I did, Blake would think that I was a prude, or, worse, that I didn't want to kiss him! If I weren't so inexperienced, this wouldn't bother me.

Blake seemed so sophisticated; he had probably kissed a thousand women in a thousand real-life scenes like this.

I knew I'd screw up this "acted" kiss. The moment Blake's experienced lips touched mine, he would know the truth. What if he tried to French kiss? I thought in horror. *What would I do*?

Antoinette could do it. She's tough. She would probably approach it professionally, the way she does karate. But how could I kiss professionally when I hadn't even done it as an amateur, yet!

I closed the script and put it under my bed and pulled out *The Thirty-Six Dramatic Situations*. This predicament was so horrible, it actually fit into *two* Situations.

The Sixth Situation—DISASTER. Georges Polti described this situation with words like catastrophe, suffering, and fear of the unforeseen.

Also, the Seventh Situation—FALLING PREY TO CRUELTY OR MISFORTUNE. Georges wrote, "Beneath that which seems the final depth of misfortune, there may open another yet more frightful." Ha, Georges, that's all you know. Nothing could be more frightful.

I slapped the little green book shut and wondered, momentarily, if I could take many more dramatic situations.

Ten

Antoinette grunted a greeting of "It's raining" to me after school on Tuesday and stuffed her books into her locker.

I wasn't in such a good mood, either. I hadn't seen Blake all day, and this bothered me. If he was searching for me, too, like he had said on the phone, surely our combined efforts would have had some result. But, I told myself, he could be working like a madman to find me, and our paths just never crossed. Stranger things have happened.

"Why don't we just go to Green Lake Drugs?" Antoinette queried. "Department store make-up is a rip-off."

"Because I want sophisticated, *nice* stuff. Besides, Nordstrom's has all those charts and perfume samplers. And salespeople to tell you what looks good."

Antoinette rolled her eyes. "MacBeth, how much money do you have?"

"Ten dollars."

"If you can get two things for that, I'll be shocked."

"If I'm as gorgeous as you say, I'll only need two things," I reasoned. The bus roared up at that moment.

On the way to Northgate shopping mall, I told Antoinette about the script disaster.

"Sounds fun to me," she said. "Just roll with it, Mac-Beth. You'll be able to tell when his kiss stops being acted and becomes real."

"I suppose you're the voice of experience," I said sarcastically.

"I have an imagination," she said and smiled.

The shadowy, sexy lighting in the Nordstrom's cosmetics department made it particularly intriguing. And everything was so clean. Rows of silver-capped bottles reflected off sparkling clear glass displays, mirrors and glossy floors. I instantly felt dowdy and plain, but the objective here, I reminded myself, was to rub some of this glitz onto me.

Antoinette wasn't the slightest bit intimidated and marched over to a display box with graphs and levers. "Okay," she said. "Let's figure out what season you are."

"Season?"

"Sure!" Antoinette said. I had no idea she was so well versed in make-up. "My mother," she explained, "never goes shopping without her pack of acceptable colors. She's Spring. I'm Winter. I bet you're Autumn."

"You're right!" a very blond, highly blushed person enthused from the other side of the glass counter. "Redheads are almost always Autumns, unless they're Springs."

"I have *auburn* hair," I corrected.

"Of course you do, dear," she acknowledged. She adjusted a tall silver extension lamp over me and peered into my eyes. "Ummmm. Hazel. Now *think*, dear." She pointed her long, perfectly polished red fingernail to her head. Was she instructing me in brain identification, or what?

"*Think*," she repeated. "What colors does your wardrobe mainly consist of? Blue or yellow undertones?"

"I wear a lot of black," I replied.

A frown creased the woman's smooth forehead. "Only Winters can wear black. You may wear a little black, but you need *warmer* colors. Bronze and rust."

Gee thanks, I thought, and gave Antoinette a forlorn look. Antoinette laughed.

"Girls! Down here!" our salesperson beckoned. I wondered if she was on roller skates, she moved so quickly. "Let me show you." She pointed to a tray of pots that had words like *creamy* and *lustrous* on their tiny name plates. There were three categories: Traditional (which had a lot of boring browns), Adventurous (full of pinky oranges), and Poetic (predominantly purples).

"This is Summer," she said positively, pointing at the Adventurous pinky-orange blush. Then she cocked her head to one side. "Or I suppose it could be Spring, if you warmed it up."

"Spring is warmer than Summer?" I asked, confused.

"Why, yes, of course, dear!" she said, placing her hands flat on the countertop, like a person sure of her fact. "This is cool, this is warm." She pointed at the appropriate pots. "Cool, warm, cool, warm. Think. Cool, warm." She smiled.

"Cool, warm," Antoinette and I said in unison.

"You are cool," the woman said, pointing to Antoinette, "and you," she said, pointing to me, "are warm." Somehow I knew that this meant I didn't get the passionate, poetic purples.

"You are Poetic." The fingernail pointed to a dejected Antoinette.

Then the woman focused on me. "You are Adventurous."

I blinked. "I am?"

"Absolutely. But you can wear some of these warmer Traditional browns, if you'd like."

I wanted to hug her, but she didn't seem so inclined. "So what would you like to try?"

"How much is this Adventurous blush?" I pointed to the bronze-colored pot labeled "Heartbeat."

"Six dollars." She brushed some on my cheek. "Absolutely exquisite!" I thought of how perfectly matched this saleswoman would be with Dash Honeycutt, but I decided not to set them up. If they ended up liking each other, she could be my mother-in-law.

"Oh. Well, how much is your smallest pot of French blue eyeshadow?" I asked.

"One size fits all, dear!" she said, and burst out laughing. "Three dollars. Plus tax, of course. Here, try some on." She handed me a pencil with a blue tip. "Just draw a line above your eyelashes! It comes with its very own sharpener, absolutely free!"

I drew the line, consulted the mirror, and sighed with relief. I am Adventurous! I thought happily to myself. "Okay. I'll take them."

"Excellent choices! These are such lovely colors! And what would you like?" she asked Antoinette.

"Nothing, thanks."

The merest scowl tugged at the saleswoman's mouth. "Oh." She selected two small boxes from behind a mirror. "I'll ring these up down here, dear."

"I'll ring her up," Antoinette murmured, and we both giggled. With my accent and my Adventurous new make-up, the flame of love would surely be sparked in Blake's heart, and he could forget all of his troubles forever!

At home, I had barely had time to change my clothes when Ferguson came over. He had come straight from the theater. "Blake was kicked off the stage crew today," he reported. "He showed up late with Dean Boswell."

"Kicked off?" I echoed. "His father *fired* him?"

"Yeah. Dash hates it when people are late, and he'd already given Blake several warnings."

"Dash always picks on Blake," I blurted angrily.

Ferguson raised his eyebrows in surprise. I looked away.

"Dean asked me to cover for them," Ferguson continued. "I was supposed to say that I had seen them arrive on time and that they were busy with some props off-stage. Needless to say, I didn't do it."

For a moment I was mad at Ferguson for not covering, but the amazing and scary thought that Ferguson would stand up to Dean doused my anger. I still felt defensive, though. "Dean is hanging around Blake, probably trying to coerce him into his group of hoods," I said indignantly. "Can't Dash see that? He's driving Blake right into Dean's hands."

"Dash didn't fire Blake until Blake started talking back to him. Then, when Dash told him to get out, Blake told him that was the best news he'd ever heard and slammed out of the theater."

I groaned.

"Blake yelled that he's going back to San Francisco," Ferguson said.

"When?" I asked, panicked. I saw my whole future leaving on a DC10.

Ferguson shrugged. "He just said that at least he got his end of the deal, whatever that means, and stomped out of the theater with Dean."

I didn't know what Blake meant about a deal, either. He hadn't mentioned any deal to me.

"Dean's in our English class," Ferguson continued. "I think he's having lots of trouble at home, too, so they got to talking."

"*Dean*," I growled.

Ferguson nodded. "Yeah."

I thought about Antoinette's ad, and how she could

end up going to the dance with Dean, or someone equally scuzzy. "I wonder if Dean is going to the dance Friday night," I mumbled.

"I hope not," Ferguson said. "I'd rather not bump into him so soon, if you know what I mean."

"You're going to the dance?"

"Yes. I've even got a date." He smiled grandly.

I smiled back, but I didn't feel like talking about the dance. Blake was in trouble.

Ferguson must have sensed this because he shut up and we both sat quietly on the living-room couch, considering these horrible events.

Then I stood up, and Ferguson followed me into the kitchen for some chocolate milk. We drank silently. Ferguson was unusually quiet. Maybe he was remembering his own parents' divorce, I thought. Maybe he was worrying about what Dean might do to him. Maybe he was feeling sad about Blake. Whatever it was, it didn't last long.

"Moooo!" he wailed in true cow fashion. He set his empty glass on the counter and left me to worry about Blake. I recalled the Seventh Situation—FALLING PREY TO CRUELTY OR MISFORTUNE. Just yesterday I had scoffed at Georges's prediction that there might be a more frightful misfortune than the script kiss. I had been wrong.

Eleven

It was Wednesday, only one more day until Blake-Day, and I desperately needed to talk to someone about the script. And not Antoinette or Ferguson.

Then I remembered Mom. She would know what to do. I knocked on the door of the study. "Come in-ski," came Mom's voice.

"What did you say?" I asked, opening the door.

"It's my Russian accent." she grinned. "Can't you tell?"

"Actually, no," I replied as kindly as I could. She sounded quite ridiculous.

"Dillman just discovered the horrible truth about what the Russians have planned."

"Which is?" I asked.

still working on that part," Mom sighed. She removed the pencil that balanced behind her ear and stretched. "I'll figure it out."

"I know you will."

"That's exactly what Dash said to me when he called." She half-closed her eyes and mimicked Dash's husky voice. "Di, *darling,* you're a *genius.* I know you'll finish it soon." Mom rolled her eyes.

"Look what else he's done." I handed her the humiliating script.

"What's this?"

"The *Dracula* script."

I sank down into the other chair in Mom's office—the one she naps in. "Remember I told you that Blake is coming over tomorrow?"

"How could I forget? You practically asked us to relocate to California for the afternoon."

"Well, I've decided you can stay around."

"Why the sudden change?"

I handed her the script. "Read Act two, scene three."

Mom looked puzzled but took the script. She read. I sat in the Nap Chair and chewed my already stubby fingernails. Mom read on. I studied the back of her beat-up desk that Dad had bought from his old fraternity house. She had put tape over some of the words carved into the wood, in an effort to protect Katie and me, but we had long ago lifted the tape. Or, rather, Katie did the lifting and then dragged me in to see.

Mom laughed out loud and turned the page. I shifted in the Nap Chair and tried to concentrate on the posters Mom had pinned on her office walls. The posters advertised Mom's plays that had been produced in New York. Some of them had photos of actors and actresses looking serious and intense. I didn't see Dash Honeycutt.

Finally, Mom closed the script. "Cute," she said, smiling.

"Mom! Dracula comes into that girl's bed in the middle of the night and bites her neck!"

"That is part of the story of Dracula, MacBeth. The part that's different is where they end up kissing, and she bites him back!" She laughed.

"Clearly you do not understand why I asked you to read those scenes," I said primly.

"How could I? You just told me to read."

I tried to make my voice even. "Mother," I began, "that is what I'm going to read with Blake tomorrow afternoon."

"Ohhhh," she said, "I get it now. You aren't comfortable with that kind of scene, right?"

Sometimes I wonder if my mother was ever fifteen years old. "It's just so *embarrassing,*" I explained. "I've never kissed a guy, and I'm supposed to seduce Blake Honeycutt in this scene!" I looked at my watch. "In exactly twenty-four hours!" The horror of the situation once again engulfed me.

Mom still studied the script. "Hmmm," she said. "I see your point." She took a long swallow of decaf coffee. I guessed that the coffee was cold, and I had noticed a couple flecks of pencil eraser floating in it, but Mom didn't flinch.

"Don't get me wrong," I amended. " I am very attracted to Blake." I didn't know exactly how to illustrate the depth of my feeling so Mom would take me seriously. "Uh, well," I stammered, "there's nothing in this world I'd rather do than kiss him, Mom."

She didn't seem shocked by my bluntness. "But you'd rather not do it to a script," she surmised.

"Well, yeah. I mean, it's not real. It's a *performance*. How will I be able to know if he's kissing *me* or some stupid actress in a play!"

Mom chuckled. "You don't want a professional kiss, right?"

"Exactly." What I want, I thought, is for Blake to ask me to the dance, on a *normal* date, and then to kiss me. Was that so much to ask?

We were both silent as we considered the magnitude of the situation. Finally Mom said, "It's okay to skip the kissing parts. Actors do it all the time when they're learning lines."

"Really?" I hoped that Blake knew that also.

She nodded.

Relief gushed over me. That's what I needed to hear. What I didn't need to hear was Katie stampeding down the hall with Laurie Lottman. I met the two pink-cheeked Girl Scouts at the door. Katie smacked right into me.

"Watch out!" I shouted.

Katie and Laurie burst into giggles. "Sorry." Katie looked about as sorry as Mom had looked eating the Snickers—not exactly genuine regret.

"Laurie's mom said it was all right for Laurie to help me fix the dinner tomorrow *and* and spend the night!" Katie shrieked.

I recoiled. "You're both going to be here tomorrow afternoon?"

"My sister Lucy has her therapy appointment tomorrow," Laurie said. "Then Mom's taking her out to dinner, so they can talk about dumb stuff like *loving yourself*." Laurie and Katie looked at each other, then exploded into spasms of giggling.

"*Mother*," I pleaded.

"It'll be okay, MacBeth. Katie and Laurie will be in the kitchen all afternoon, won't you, girls?"

Katie put on her fake innocent face. "MacBeth and Blake won't even know we're around," she said. Mom didn't see the gleeful glance Laurie shot Katie.

"You see?" Mom said to me. "And your dad and I will be working in here."

I glared at Katie. "And no spying," I decreed.

"Scout's honor." She pointed three fingers toward the ceiling.

"What about you?" I said, eyeing Laurie.

"Me, too," she said hastily and joined Katie in the Scout salute.

I stared both of them down for at least fifteen seconds, daring them to betray their true intentions. Neither cracked a smile. They were probably biting their tongues.

"Okay," I said grudgingly. "But if I catch either of you, you will rue the day you were born."

Katie and Laurie looked at each other in bewilderment. "What does that mean?" Katie asked. Mom laughed.

"You just better not spy on Blake and me or you'll find out," I said. It occurred to me that that was a perfectly divine parting line, so I furrowed my eyebrows, shot them both a final malevolent glare, and exited, stage left, out of the study.

"What's that on your fingernails?" Dad asked as I grabbed my books off the kitchen table the next morning. "It looks like you just skinned a deer."

"DAD. How gross. It's some of Antoinette's mother's old fingernail polish. She got it before she knew she was a Spring."

"Oh. What's that smell?"

"What smell?"

"I'm not sure. Peppermint, chicory, sweet basil?" He sniffed my hair. "It's your hair, MacBeth. Your hair smells like chicory."

"Wild Sensation," I said. "My new creme rinse."

"You should try a little of that on your compost pile, Diana." He continued his teasing in TV commercial style. "Or you can use it as liquid fertilizer. Forget manure. Forget rotting vegetable matter. Wild Sensation has it all beat, hands down, for a lustrous, healthy harvest."

"Ha ha, very funny. Blake's coming home with me this afternoon, remember," I said.

"I remember." Mom said, and I shut the door.

Today was the day. I had gotten up at six o'clock to get ready. After laboring all last evening, I had come up with the correct ensemble. Ruffled calico skirt, Gunne Sax blouse, and sandals. The outfit looked like it belonged on the costume rack for a production of *Okla-*

homa!, but once I had it on, it was okay. The hair make-up and nails took me forty-five minutes. But it was worth it. I was adventurous and sophisticated. Blake didn't stand a chance.

Twelve

I watched the clock throughout every class, and I ate alone; Antoinette was meeting with Mr. Erlich and the Vice Principal about the karate club, and Ferguson was doing some computer club thing. It seemed like the only outside interest *I* had was Blake. But he was all I needed or wanted.

By the time school let out, my palms were dripping, I had nervously picked away the polish on three finger-nails, and my very own hair was asphyxiating me. Blake and I had agreed to meet in front of my homeroom at three o'clock. I rushed there after my last class, and stood next to the water fountain. Blake was late.

Three-fifteen, and still no Blake. The halls were almost empty now. I picked another fingernail clean. Three-twenty and no Blake. Was he okay? I wondered briefly. It is always best to consider a person's welfare before becoming livid.

At 3:25 I was livid. I didn't know if I even wanted to see Blake when I saw him open the hall door and saunter toward me. What if he didn't apologize or offer any explanation? What would I do then? How could I pretend that it was no big deal, and go on as if nothing had happened? I couldn't look myself in the eye again if I did that. I prayed that Blake would have an excuse.

He wore the same outfit that he had worn that night with his father. Only this time he had on a Levi's jeans jacket. I wondered if he owned another tee shirt. But I quickly dismissed that negative thought. Blake was as handsome as ever. My lividness had gone limp.

"I'm late," he said immediately. "Sorry." I waited for an explanation, but he offered none. Instead, he said, "Let's go."

A poster advertising the dance hung on the door he pushed open. Maybe he didn't see it. Maybe he didn't even *know* about the dance, for Pete's sake. It was my duty, as a veteran of the school, to alert him to these affairs.

"Say, did you see that sign, eh Blake? The first dance, 'tis tomorrow night."

Blake smiled. "I saw it," he said with undisguised amusement.

I felt pressure to make an excuse. "I just thought I'd make sure you knew what was goin' on at the school, you bein' new and all."

"Thanks, MacBeth."

Why doesn't he ask me, I wondered frantically? Maybe the accent is too much for him. Maybe he

100

doesn't like my new cheeks and eyes. I can't do much about the make-up, short of taking a dip in the lake, but I can drop the accent. Not everyone is turned on by cockney.

We walked away from the school and approached Green Lake. I picked nervously at my six fingernails that still had polish. A sailboarder on the lake fell off his bright, crayon-red sailboard. I cleared my throat.

"I heard about your dad kicking you off the stage crew," I said sympathetically. "That was so unfair."

"Yeah," Blake said. "But typical." He was watching the sailboarder.

I desperately wanted to know if he was going back to San Francisco because of the fight, but couldn't bring myself to hear the response. I just couldn't bear it if he said he was leaving. It would be better to win his heart tonight, get him to ask me to the dance tomorrow night, and *then* whisper into his ear as he kissed me, "You don't really want to go back to San Francisco, do you?"

The rest of the way home, we talked about the art of sailboarding, and Blake told me a long story about his friend's sailboat, in San Francisco. And then he told me another long story about his last basketball game, in San Francisco. I got a little tired of the words "in San Francisco," but I figured listening to them was a small courtesy to give the one you love.

When we walked in the front door, the air was heavy with steam and the smell of fried onions. A large sign was taped to the kitchen door: DO NOT ENTER—

THIS MEANS YOU! I smiled at Blake and peeked inside. From the back, Katie looked like the Wizard of Oz at his smoking control panel, frantically trying to pull the right levers and push the right buttons. She stood at the stove cooking dinner. Laurie sat at the kitchen sink, peeling carrots.

The kitchen was a disaster area. Dirty pots and pans filled the sink, some sort of dough blanketed the kitchen table, every measuring device Mom owned littered the counters, and at least three pots bubbled on the stove in front of our hostess.

Quietly I backed out and noticed that there was more to Katie's sign than just the warning.

CHEAP BUT NUTRITIOUS MEAL GUEST LIST
Mom and Dad
Blake and MacBeth
Lee and Antoinette
Ferguson and Laurie

I blushed at the second entry. Blake just strolled into the living room, dropped onto the couch, and slid his script onto the coffee table. I guess he was also embarrassed by the sign. Probably he didn't trust himself to linger next to me since Katie was so near.

I sat next to him on the couch and waited. This was a perfect time for him to hold my hand, to rub my neck again, to tell me how much he longed for me.

"Let's get started," he said, and picked up the script.

"Okay." Work first, I thought, then pleasure.

Blake started reading, moving his finger under the line.

> BLAKE: (*Monotone.*) Don't be afraid. I won't hurt you. Come closer to me.
> ME: Where did you come from?
> BLAKE: Relax. (*Long, inappropriate pause.*) Just relax.
> ME: What are you doing?

Blake was reading his lines as though they were from the Seattle phone book. But, I reminded myself, *I* was the one auditioning. Blake never actually *said* he was an actor.

Creak. Creak, creak. The kitchen door. Someone was at the kitchen door. And I noticed that all the banging had stopped.

> BLAKE: Relax. Just relax.
> ME: I asked you what you think you're *doing!*
> BLAKE: We were meant for each other. (*pause.*) Look (*pause*) into my *eyes.*

I peeked at him without turning my head, to see if he expected me to actually look into his eyes. He didn't. Whew.

> ME: We are practically strangers!

BLAKE: What does that matter! Now that
I've found you, I'll never let you go!

Blake read the lines very slowly, as if he were Matt Dillon in an episode of "Gunsmoke," warning a horse thief not to even think of busting out of his jail. But it was still Blake's voice. And it was still Blake saying those words to me! I felt my cheeks getting hot. The rest of the room seemed to fade away. It was the chemistry again. Sizzling, popping, making me crazy.

Creak, from the kitchen door.

ME: (*Shrieking.*) Oh! How dare you!
BLAKE: (*Droning.*) I'm crazy about you.

Oh, brother, I thought. The kissing part is only one line away!

ME: I love you, too! I can't fight it any
longer!

Blake rubbed his chin and grinned. "Let's skip this part, okay?"

"Sure," I said, relieved. "I'm dying of thirst. Do you want some Kool-Aid?"

"Yeah." He didn't look up. He was just as embarrassed as I was!

As I walked toward the kitchen, I saw a flash of movement on the stairs. A moment later, the door to Katie's room clicked shut.

Blake and I read through the scene a couple more times, Blake digressing only once into a San Francisco story, and then he went into the kitchen to check on dinner. He did not ask me to the dance, even though I gave him ample opportunity. I couldn't figure the boy out. He had acted so interested. So wasn't a date to the dance only logical?

The doorbell rang. It was Antoinette, and she looked quite cute. No karate *Gi* tonight. She had on a tight jeans skirt, a baggy pink and turquoise polo shirt that came down over the top of the skirt, and soft loafers. Her hair was brushed back and she had on pale pink lipstick.

"You look great," I said.

"Thanks. Does my hair look okay?" She examined herself in the hall mirror. "It's still moussed."

"It's fine. Really."

Antoinette whirled around to face me. "You won't believe the letter the Scoundrel sent me!" she cried. But before she could dig it out of her pocket, the doorbell rang.

"Show it to me later, okay?" She nodded.

I opened the door and Aunt Leah fluttered into the house in a red silk dress. She fussed with her handbag (she never calls it a purse), umbrella, and sweater, which all hung on her left forearm. Katie ran out to greet her. A Vile Kyle tape blared from the kitchen.

"Hello, Aunt Leah. I'm glad you could make it."

"Thank you, MacBeth . . . Diana . . . I mean *Katie*."

She always names every niece before she hits the right one.

Katie smiled politely. "This is Laurie, my friend from school. You know Antoinette. And this is MacBeth's friend, Blake. This is Aunt Leah."

"Hi," Laurie said.

Antoinette smiled and waved.

"Hi," Blake mumbled and looked down at his hands. He couldn't read very well, I had to admit, but he was so very gallant. And I'd experienced more dramatic situations in the week I'd known him than in the entire fifteen years before.

"Nice to meet you both," Aunt Leah said. And then she sniffed. "Smells like homemade biscuits to me! Heavenly!"

Katie was asking Aunt Leah what she would like to drink when the front doorbell rang again. "Excuse me," Katie said primly. "That's probably Laurie's date." She let Ferguson in. Aunt Leah looked a little shocked. Ferguson *was* much older than Laurie. "Oh my," she said.

Ferguson's braces were off, and his friendly smile was noticeably clean and straight. And his glasses were gone! He must have gotten contacts. I hardly recognized him.

He wore a tan corduroy sports coat and a tie, and his hair was cut. It even looked like a *bought* haircut. Even I had to admit that he looked great.

"These are for you, Katie. You look lovely." Ferguson handed Katie a bouquet of pink roses and she blushed wildly, her cheeks blending into her peach-colored alligator polo dress.

She graciously took the flowers and, since Ferguson already knew everybody, she invited us all into the dining room. "Dinner is served," she announced.

My name plate, printed in a rainbow of felt-tip pen colors, sat between Blake's and Dad's.

We both looked down at our plates and saw a menu card.

THE LANGLEY HAPPY KITCHEN
One Gourmet Dinner

One serving Offal Stew	$.30
One serving Ratatouille	$.25
35 Buttered Peas	$.10
Two Homemade Biscuits	$.15
Honey and Butter	
(One tablespoon each)	$.10
One serving Red Jell-O	$.10
TOTAL PER PERSON	$1.00

When I looked up, everyone's head was bowed and I thought they were saying grace. Actually, I was the first to finish reading the menu and to absorb its full meaning. Katie smiled proudly from the head of the table.

Dad pointed to the menu. "What's offal?" he murmured to me out the side of his mouth.

"Beats me," I murmured back. "I'm wondering what's in *ratatouille*." Dad smiled.

"Everything looks great, Katie!" Ferguson said. Blake nodded. He seemed to be having a good time. Surely his instincts were telling him that life with me would be totally unpredictable, like this dinner. It was our destiny. How could he leave it?

"Oh, my, yes!" Aunt Leah agreed. "So many colors. Very pleasing to the eye."

"And so reasonably priced." Dad surveyed the menu again. "Are you open for business every weekend?"

Katie giggled. "Come on, Daddy! Start eating. Everything is getting cold."

And so we passed the dishes. The offal stew looked suspiciously like wads of already chewed Wrigley's gum in a cream sauce. I recognized chunks of zucchini and eggplant in the *ratatouille*. It was hard to believe that these were the choices of a fifth-grader. I noticed that Katie and Laurie took minuscule helpings of the offal stew.

Blake ate voraciously. I tried to catch his eye, to have a special moment between us, but he was more interested in the food. Passionate scenes have different effects on different people, I reasoned.

When every bowl was scraped clean, Aunt Leah begged Katie for the offal stew recipe. "I don't know why it's called *offal*," she commented. "That sounds so much like *awful*, and it's absolutely divine!"

"What is in the offal stew, Katie?" Mom asked as she licked some *ratatouille* from her lips.

Katie balked. Laurie giggled.

"I don't know if I should tell," Katie said.

"Don't be one of those secretive cooks," admonished my father.

"Yeah," Ferguson agreed. "Tell us, Katie. Maybe I could even make it."

"Well . . ." Katie looked at Laurie, who was still giggling. "Do you all promise not to get mad?"

In unison, we demanded, "WHAT WAS IN THE STEW, KATIE?"

"I asked the butcher at the store for the cheapest meat he had," explained Katie. "He said that he could give me three pounds of offal, *practically free*. So I took it."

"And we ate it," Mom said. "For the last time, Kathryn Elaine Langley, *what is offal*?

"Livers, brains, and tails."

"Livers, brains, and *tails*?" echoed my father.

Katie nodded. "Livers, brains, and tails."

"Oh, my," sighed Aunt Leah.

Thirteen

Everyone was stunned by Katie's revelation. And then Ferguson started laughing. He laughed in his old, friendly way, relieving the tension and making things fun. He really did have a good sense of humor.

The adults were still making offal jokes when they took their coffee into the living room, to talk. Katie and Laurie went upstairs, to giggle, and Ferguson, Antoinette, Blake, and I cleared the dining-room table, to play Clue, my favorite game.

"I'm thirsty," said Ferguson. "Does either of you lovely ladies want some liquid refreshment?"

"No, thanks," we said simultaneously.

"I'll go with you," Blake said.

"Hey," Antoinette whispered to me, "have you noticed Ferguson isn't so bad-looking tonight?"

"He looks like plain old Ferguson to me," I answered casually.

Why am I lying to her? I asked myself. I'm lying to her because I don't know what's going on inside of me. So what if Ferguson is attractive tonight? *I* love Blake. He is the one who's turning my life around.

Ferguson and Blake returned with glasses of milk and the game began. Antoinette said that she wanted to be the sexy Miss Scarlet. Ferguson chose Professor Plum, Blake was Colonel Mustard, and I decided on Mrs. Peacock, since she reminded me of Agatha Christie. My feelings were so confused this evening, I just wanted to escape up into my room and into a good mystery.

We started playing. On his third move, Ferguson said to Antoinette, chuckling. "So how many guys have you flipped, Antoinette?"

"I wouldn't laugh if I were you," Antoinette responded. "I've sparred with lots of guys your size, and won."

"Is that so?" Ferguson said.

"This I've got to see," Blake commented.

Antoinette froze, her hand poised above her Miss Scarlet marker. "You sound as if you don't believe me." She smiled wryly at the two boys.

"Oh, I believe you," Ferguson responded. "You're shorter than I, which gives you a lower center of gravity."

"I'm just plain stronger than you are, Ferguson. Or you, Blake." Antoinette had thrown down the gauntlet in her own, flirtatious way, and Ferguson, being Ferguson, could do nothing but pick it up.

Meanwhile, I sat quietly, feeling the strange and startling beginnings of jealousy.

"You really think you're stronger?" Ferguson was asking. "Women's upper body strength is generally much less than men's."

"Does either of you want to arm wrestle?"

Blake put his hands up in a "No way" gesture.

"You're sure you want to, Antoinette?" Ferguson asked.

Antoinette moved over close to Ferguson. Now I was definitely, full-fledged, hideously jealous. There was no other word for my sudden impulse to kill Antoinette. What was wrong with me? I was losing my mind.

I watched as they positioned themselves, Antoinette's black hair brushing against Ferguson's cheek as she adjusted the height of her arm. They clasped hands.

"Ready?" Antoinette asked.

"Ready," Ferguson answered.

"The battle of the sexes," Blake said and laughed. I love *you*, I love *you*, I chanted to myself and stared at Blake.

"I'll say 'go'," I announced.

"Okay," said Antoinette.

I waited until they were both perfectly still, and then said, "Ready, set, GO!"

The battle was on. Both hands quivered, both contestants looked constipated, their faces growing red with the effort. It seemed to be a tie for the first fifteen seconds, but then, slowly, Antoinette's weightlifting began to pay off. Inch by inch she forced Ferguson's arm lower and lower until SMACK! The back of Ferguson's wrist landed flat on the table.

"Wow!" Ferguson cried. "You've got quite an arm on you! I don't know if I'll ever be the same!" Antoinette glowed with pleasure.

"Now that the gymnastics are over," I said, "can we get on with the game?"

"Indeed," Ferguson replied, and looked at me with a funny expression on his face. Antoinette moved back to her place, and we played in silence for several minutes. I pretended to concentrate.

When it was Ferguson's turn, he accused me of killing Mr. Boddy in the ballroom with the wrench. I quickly produced the wrench card and said, "Wrong. Nyah nyah." That was my feeble attempt at flirting. I was still in third grade when it came to relationships, I realized.

Ferguson laughed and reached over to the ballroom to replace my blue marker. I had reached for it a second earlier. Ferguson's hand landed on mine and lingered there for the merest moment. I let myself feel his large, warm hand over mine and my heart soared.

"Nyah nyah yourself," Ferguson quipped, but all I could see in his familiar face was good-natured laughter. Ferguson carried on with the game as if nothing had happened between us. And really, MacBeth, I told myself, haven't you had enough of fantasized feelings? You are an emotional wreck.

Still, I couldn't get Ferguson out of my mind. I noticed little things about him that I had never noticed before. When he crossed his legs, the leg that crossed was so long that his no-name sneaker brushed the floor.

Who else but Ferguson would wear sneakers with a sports coat? He was smart enough to make up his own style.

I noticed how nicely his watch looked on his wrist, nestled into a few longish dark hairs. I wondered if he had very many of those longish dark hairs on his chest?

Once, when it was Antoinette's turn, Ferguson rubbed his eyes. The new contacts were bugging him. He looked at me, and I knew he couldn't see me very well, but I smiled. My smile said, "Do I like you, Ferguson Alphonse Parrish?" I knew he couldn't see it.

We were just starting our second game when we heard Katie and Laurie in the kitchen. The swinging door between the kitchen and the dining room was closed, and we were quietly concentrating on the game, so Katie and Laurie didn't realize we were there. They started cleaning up the kitchen, and, cruel fate, we could hear every word they said.

LAURIE: (*Giggling.*) Let's play like we're Lucy and Mike.
KATIE: (*Over the sound of running water.*) We always play Lucy and her boyfriends. Let's play MacBeth and Blake.
LAURIE: You mean like this afternoon?
KATIE: Yeah! I want to be Blake.
LAURIE: Okay. I'm MacBeth. (*Cabinet door*

	slamming.) You start.
KATIE:	(*Fake deep voice*.) Don't be afraid. I won't hurt you. Come closer to me.
LAURIE:	(*Giggling*.) What are you doing!
KATIE:	(*Very dramatic*.) Relax, just *re-laaaax*.
LAURIE:	If you don't leave I'm going to scream!

By now, Antoinette, Ferguson, and Blake had realized what was going on in the kitchen and were listening with interest. Antoinette looked at me with raised eyebrows, Ferguson's mouth hung open, and Blake blushed.

"Hey, Katie! *Knock that off*!" I yelled, but she didn't hear me. Laurie had banged a pot and drowned me out.

"Shhhh," said Ferguson urgently. "This is very interesting." He looked upset. Katie and Laurie continued on unmercifully.

KATIE:	We were meant for each other. I'll never let you go!
LAURIE:	We are practically strangers!
KATIE:	I'm not positive, but didn't Blake say something like "I'm crazy about you?"
LAURIE:	Yeah. And then MacBeth said "I love you, too. I can't fight it any longer."

115

The two actresses started laughing hysterically. Antoinette cringed visibly and tried to smother a giggle, and Blake squirmed; neither was listening to my explanation. Ferguson was bright red.

I realized in a flash that this moment was the absolute nadir of my existence. Things simply could get no worse.

When the doorbell rang at that precise moment, I seized the opportunity to escape. My parents and Aunt Leah were still sipping and chatting. I jogged through the living room and opened the front door. It was pouring rain.

I swallowed deeply. "Dean," I said. He stood on the porch, one hand resting on the side of our house, trying to look studly.

"I'm here to get Blake," Dean announced.

"Blake?" I echoed.

"Yeah. He told me he'd be here."

"Uh, just a second. I'll get him."

But Blake was right beside me. "Hi," he said to Dean. "I just have to get the script I brought over." They really were *friends*, I realized. How could this be?

"I'll get it," I offered. I didn't want Dean to follow Blake inside, and I needed to get away from Dean. I couldn't think straight around him.

I ran to get the *Dracula* manuscript off the coffee table, and when I returned, Blake was out on the porch talking with Dean. They didn't see me.

"Why are you still making up to her?" Dean asked.

"You get to move back to 'Frisco because you got your

old man the information he wanted about her mom's play, right?"

What was he talking about? What information? I moved closer to the door, to hear better. It sounded like they were talking about *me*.

"Shhh," Blake said. "Yeah, the deal's over. Dad wants to direct Mrs. Langley's new play, or maybe get her to write in a good part for him. He needed to know how far along she was so he could know when to make his move."

"You're lucky MacBeth played right into your hands," Dean said.

I wanted to throw up when Blake grunted "You can say that again" to Dean.

Blake had *acted* interested in me so he could spy on Mom for Dash.

If they had discovered me eavesdropping at that moment, I'm sure they would have taken me for a corpse.

Everything made sense. This treachery was probably hatched in Dash's head the second he heard Mom mention her new play. I remembered his looking at me that night over dessert, how he noticed my interest in Blake. He had plotted the whole thing right then.

No wonder Blake had called me so unexpectedly to audition. No wonder he had been so interested in my mother. *Not* because he was gallant. And Blake hadn't asked me to the dance because he didn't need me anymore.

The two creeps were talking again.

"So why are you here now?" Dean asked. Good ques-

117

tion, I thought.

"I'd already said I'd help her practice," Blake explained. "You know, the *love scene*."

Dean chortled. "Yeah. How'd it go?"

"Okay. She's not such a bad kid."

Yeah, I'm not such a bad kid, so why did you use me? How ruthless can you be? How selfish and deceitful?

"Did you get hold of your mom?" Dean asked.

"Yeah, and she understood. She knows what Dad is like. I can leave as soon as I want."

The sooner the better, I wanted to shout. This kind of dramatic situation I didn't need.

Just then Ferguson walked into the hallway. Dean and Blake heard him and looked up. "*You*," Dean snarled. "The fink that got Blake fired."

"Hi," Ferguson said. "So nice to see you, Dean. Looks real wet out there."

Dean pushed his tongue against his cheek and looked at Ferguson with steely eyes. He drummed his fingers on the mailbox. "You better not get in my way, *fink*," he sneered.

I felt blood rush to my head. Ferguson said nothing. *I* said nothing.

Blake said "Come on" to Dean. Dean glared at Ferguson one last time. "*Watch out*," he said.

I shoved the *Dracula* script I'd been clutching into Blake's hand, and he sauntered down the sidewalk with Dean.

I closed the door. Antoinette, Ferguson, and I stood

in the hallway like statues, puzzling over this turn of events.

"Dean's a jerk," Antoinette finally commented. "Don't worry about him, Ferguson. He's all talk."

Ferguson shrugged. "I don't care about Dean," he said. Then he looked directly at me, and my legs got wobbly. "According to what Katie and Laurie heard, you had a real date with Blake this afternoon. And without my help. Congratulations."

"That kiss . . ." I began.

But for once in his life, Ferguson didn't want to talk. "Look," he mumbled, "I've got to go home." He took three long strides to the kitchen door, stuck his head in and said thanks to Katie, and then left.

I sank against the door. I was too overcome to explain what a slime Blake had turned out to be. Blake might be a perfect physical specimen, but his heart stank.

And it looked like any chance I might have had with Ferguson was dust in the wind. And rain.

Antoinette noticed my condition. "Don't worry about it, MacBeth. Dean really is all talk. But it's weird that Blake is *friends* with him."

"Actually, it's not so weird," I said. I took her up to my room and explained the whole miserable story.

"Scum of the earth," Antoinette concluded.

I nodded.

"Hey, I've got something that will cheer you up!" She pulled a paper out of her pocket. "It's from the Scoundrel."

Dear Enchantress,

    Scoundrels do not answer questionnaires.

    It's time to get down to business. Since you are so intrigued with Jane Austen's book, *Sense and Sensibility*, I propose the following method of recognition.

    In the book, Marianne snips a lock of her hair and gives it to her sweetheart, Willoughby, as a romantic gift. Snip a lock of your hair, tie it in a ribbon, and pin it to your shoulder Friday at the dance. I will do likewise. Let me know in the usual manner if you agree to this.

"Can you believe this guy?" Antoinette asked.

I shook my head. "No, I can't," said. Whoever the Scoundrel might be, I was pretty sure now that it wasn't Dean, or one of his hoods. Dean would never wear hair pinned to his shoulder.

"Listen," Antoinette continued, "I've already got a date to the dance. Greg, this guy at karate, asked me, so I can't meet the Scoundrel. You don't have a date, though. Why don't you be the Enchantress?"

"Forget it," I said. But then I thought of Blake's treachery, and I started to fume. No way was he going to ruin my chances for true love this year. "Well . . . okay," I said. "I'll do it." Antoinette cheered.

"Should I go along with that crazy hair scheme, though?" I asked.

"Yes. Definitely wear the hair." She giggled. "It's romantic."

Before I went to bed, on this most hideous of nights, I thumbed through *The Thirty-Six Dramatic Situations*.

This was clearly the Twenty-Seventh Situation—
DISCOVERY OF THE DISHONOR OF A LOVED
ONE. My specific case was B(7): *Discovery that One's
Lover is a Scoundrel.*

Fourteen

F riday afternoon I washed my hair and snipped a
  small lock from the back. Mom has a sewing bas-
ket she uses for mending, and I found a pink velvet
ribbon in the bottom of it. I tied the ribbon around the
lock of hair and attached a safety pin.

I blew my hair dry and fluffed it with my fingers. No
braid tonight, I decided. Scoundrels do not answer
questionnaires, and Enchantresses do not wear braids.
Besides, I could hide the ribbon under my hair until the
appropriate moment. I decided to wear the pair of dark
brown combs Katie had given me last Christmas.

Black turtleneck, batik wraparound skirt, sandals, and
a touch of Heartbeat blush and French blue eyeshadow
and I was ready, physically. Emotionally, I was a wreck.

I opened my top dresser drawer, and fished out my
THE PERFECT BOY FOR ME list. I thought of Ferguson and checked off all the items except Number 4,
Musical. And, as I had noted before, "musical" was a
stupid requirement. There was no question, Ferguson
was All of the Above, for me, anyway.

I had thought the same about Blake, though, and look what kind of person he'd turned out to be. A liar and a cheat. And, yes, a drip.

Blake had used me, but I wasn't exactly blameless. After all, I really wasn't that interested in his spiritual qualities, either.

But I couldn't think of Ferguson or Blake now. I had to concentrate on the Mystery Man and my future.

I replaced the list and picked up *The Thirty-Six Dramatic Situations*. I was sure that meeting a guy at a dance with a lock of hair pinned to your chest wasn't in the little green book, but I was wrong. There was no denying that this was the Sixteenth Situation: MADNESS.

Katie knocked hastily at my door and then stuck her head inside. She still didn't know we had overheard her and Laurie last night. But after Antoinette left, I decided that I had enough going on in my life without complicating it with murder. "I'm helping Laurie with her dinner," Katie announced cheerfully. "She helped me, so I'm helping her."

"Whether she wants it or not, right?"

"She wants it. Guess what? So far my dinner's still the cheapest!"

"I never heard what the prize is," I said. "What is it?"

"An insect collecting kit!" Katie glowed. "Complete with net, formaldehyde, and a display box with pins you stick through the bug's guts!"

"Katie!"

"It's okay, MacBeth," she assured me. "They don't feel a thing because they're already dead. I'll have my

123

insect badge in no time!" She smiled and skipped down the stairs.

Antoinette and Greg gave me a ride to the dance. I tried to run away only once, when we were in the school parking lot, but Antoinette kept a vise-like grasp on my arm.

The cafeteria had been festively decorated for the dance. Streamers and banners hung from the ceiling and walls. TRUMAN BEARS, NUMBER ONE! proclaimed one banner, DANCE THE NIGHT AWAY advised another. I recognized a guy from my history class playing in the band. Students were everywhere, trying to talk over the music, loitering against the walls, and some even dancing.

"We're going to dance," Antoinette said to me. "See you later, okay?"

"Sure, go ahead! I'm just going to hang around here for a while."

"You need some time to look for the Scoundrel, right?"

I blushed and shoved her toward the dance floor. "Go dance," I said.

Antoinette laughed and pulled Greg to the middle of the cafeteria. I watched them for a few minutes and thought I detected a couple of karate thrusts and kicks in their dancing. They smiled at each other a lot.

It was very hot, I noticed, as I scanned the cafeteria for Ferguson. There were too many bodies, and not one of them, as far as I could see, belonged to Ferguson

Parrish. Dean Boswell and a couple of his friends, not including Blake, hung around the exit, looking surly as they, too, scanned the cafeteria. Nervously, I made sure the lock on my shoulder was well hidden.

Suddenly I was blinded. A large sweaty palm from behind me masked my eyes.

"Hiya, Mac! Guess who?" boomed the familiar voice.

"Jeep Hollingsworth, get your hands off me." I pried the cupped hand off my carefully made-up eyes.

"How'd you know it was me?" Jeep crowed. He took great pride in being recognized.

Slowly I turned around. "Jeep," I said, looking up at his swollen chest and red cheeks. *"Don't ever do that again."* And then a fleck of something dropped into my eye, probably a bit of crushed eyelash or crumbled mascara, but my eyeball felt like a gravel pit. Tears welled and I blinked furiously.

"Gosh, Mac, I didn't mean to hurt you," said Jeep, in a contrite voice. "Sometimes I don't know my own strength."

I groaned. "It's not that, Jeep. I've got something in my eye!"

"Let me see. I'm good at this." He moved in close, holding my face up to his. "Turn toward the light," he instructed.

I didn't see that I had much choice but to let him search. He furrowed his brow in concentration, studying my eye at close range. I was practically overcome by the musk cologne that he must have bathed in before the dance.

Antoinette came to my rescue. The song was over, and she and Greg emerged from the crowd into the corner where Jeep and I huddled. I'm sure she was amused at my situation, but she managed to make her voice sound concerned. "What's the matter, MacBeth?"

"She's got some crud in her eye." diagnosed Jeep.

"Do you see anything? I asked impatiently.

"Hold on," Jeep instructed. "Alllll-most got it." He pulled at the skin on my temple, and I felt a stinging pressure as he stuck his finger in my eye. "*Got it!*" he cried.

I turned away and wiped wet black mascara from my cheek.

"I'm an expert at this," Jeep informed Antoinette and Greg, and presented, with a flourish, the evidence on the tip of his index finger. "See?" he said.

Antoinette ignored Jeep. "Are you okay?" she asked me.

"I'll survive," I replied. I was rubbing my eye and didn't see Ferguson approach us. Jeep stood very close to me.

"Hi, you guys. Having fun?" Ferguson gazed at me. "It doesn't look like it." He didn't sound mad, but Ferguson wasn't the type to carry a grudge. I wondered if I'd ever get the chance to explain everything to him.

"MacBeth got something in her eye," Antoinette quickly explained. "Jeep got it out for her."

"Too bad." He looked directly at Jeep. "I mean, too bad about MacBeth's eye."

I got my first real look at Ferguson through swollen

eyes. He was wearing a light blue button-down shirt, tan corduroys and a navy Nike jacket.

Ferguson seemed so handsome to me. His ears still stuck out like seashells, but I didn't mind them anymore. Next to the gruesome Jeep, who wore painfully tight jeans and a short Rock Seattle tee shirt, he was gorgeous.

Antoinette spoke up brightly. "Ferguson, I'd like you to meet Greg Spencer. We take karate together."

Ferguson nodded "hi" to Greg.

"I thought you had a date," I said.

"Don't worry, MacBeth. I'm taken care of."

"Anyone I know?" Antoinette asked.

"Probably not," Ferguson said carefully.

"Hey, Mac," Jeep blurted. "The band's starting up again. Let's dance."

"Uh," I hesitated, but Jeep apparently took any response short of "Forget it" to be assent. He seized my hand and dragged me out to dance. The band began, and Jeep started to jiggle, snapping his head up and down to the music. I averted my eyes from Jeep, and saw Ferguson dancing with Lucy Lottman. *Was Lucy Ferguson's date?*

Lucy was a terrific dancer, and she looked even more terrific dancing with Ferguson. They smiled at each other as they danced to the beat. My heart was breaking.

And then I saw Dean swagger over to them and grip Ferguson's shoulder. Lucy backed away, and Dean spoke to Ferguson and motioned toward the parking lot exit where one of his buddies hovered. Ferguson did not look thrilled.

Dean followed Ferguson out the exit.

Even without the little green book I had no trouble recognizing that this was a Dramatic Situation. Dean was going to beat up Ferguson. I just knew it.

Fifteen

Jeep seemed oblivious to me, he was so into keeping his large body under control, so I slipped away.

Outside, beyond the breezeway, stretched the parking lot and the football field. It was dark, but the moon was clear and white. A few couples leaned against cars in the parking lot, talking or making out.

Dean and one of his hoods staggered behind Ferguson, guiding him to the end of the football field nearest the parking lot. I followed at a safe distance.

I watched in horror as the two of them shoved Ferguson up against the goal post. Ferguson tried to struggle free, but Dean's friend clutched his shoulder. Dean swiped at Ferguson, but Ferguson ducked and Dean's fist slammed into the goal post. He didn't seem very coordinated as he backed away, hugging his hand and groaning. Four-letter words flowed freely.

Dean's friend socked Ferguson in the stomach, and Ferguson doubled over. I couldn't stand it anymore.

"Leave him alone!" I screamed angrily, running over to them.

Dean gazed at me and his lip curled. "Get out of here," he slurred.

"Watch out, MacBeth," Ferguson warned.

"Come to save your wimp of a boyfriend?" Dean said, and laughed. I was close enough to him now that I could smell alcohol. Dean's eyes were glazed over like doughnuts.

I felt blood rush to my head. "Shut up, Dean," I cried. "Ferguson Parrish is ten times the man you are. Twenty. Thirty. Leave him alone!"

Dean laughed hideously. "And who's going to make me? *You*?"

Anger buzzed in my head like a thousand bees. I marched over to the wavering Dean and said, my voice unusually low and furious, "Yes, me."

"This I gotta see." Dean folded his arms across his chest and smirked at me.

Front stance, I told myself. Back foot at a ninety degree angle. I stared at my opponent, and he stared, albeit a little cockeyed, back at me. His face blanched in terror as he must have realized what I was about to do.

"*Aaaaa!*" I shouted. I punched fiercely.

"AAAAAA!" My cry rang across the parking lot. I reared back, and thrust my foot at Dean's chest! For one electrifying moment, with the flood light catching the silver buckle of my sandal, I was IT. I was James Bond and Katharine Hepburn and the Enchantress all rolled into one! I could make things happen.

And then, "Arg!" I fell forward into a humiliating heap. Dean had stepped aside, and I had missed him completely.

But my spirit was not doused. I stood up and flicked the dirt off my skirt.

Ferguson gasped. He had no idea, of course, that I had been studying under Antoinette.

"*Did you see that!*" Dean queried his buddy, and then doubled over in hysterics.

I saw my chance. Dean had sacrificed his eye contact. I quickly arranged myself in the karate stance and gripped Dean's upper arm. "*AAAAA!*" I shrieked, twisted, and flung the startled, drunken Dean over my body with a perfect throw. He landed in the end zone with a thud.

There was a moment of silence, while Ferguson collected his thoughts. Dean groaned. I brushed off my hands.

"Yeah! Way to go, MacBeth!" came Antoinette's and Greg's cheers. They had arrived just in time to see Dean hit the dust.

I bowed to my *Senpai*. "*Oss*," I said.

Greg told Dean's friend to get Dean out of there, and he hastily obliged. And then Greg took Antoinette's hand and started back toward the cafeteria.

It is virtually impossible to flip a person and not mess up your hair. I turned toward Ferguson and realized that my ribbon was exposed. But his jacket was open now, and he was wearing a hair ribbon, too!

"Ferguson! You're the Scoundrel!" I blurted out. "Where was the hair on your shoulder earlier, in the cafeteria?"

Ferguson laughed. "After that rescue, MacBeth, I think you've got enough hair on your chest for the both of us."

Then he lowered his voice. "We meet at last," Ferguson said. "The Enchantress is revealed."

"And the Scoundrel. Why in the world did you call yourself a scoundrel?"

"Because girls *like* dark, mysterious scoundrels, for some bizarre reason."

"Not this girl," I said.

"I thought you were going to the dance with Blake." I shook my head. "A mistake," I said. "And Katie and Laurie overheard Blake and me reading a scene. That's what they were acting out in the kitchen."

"You and Blake were *reading a scene?*" He laughed, and I nodded miserably.

"So why did you put the ad in the paper?"

"It was Antoinette's ad then. But I helped her write it."

"Oh, MacBeth." Ferguson squeezed my arm. "I'm glad you wore the hair." I felt shivers of electricity, grand-passion-strength electricity, racing down my spine.

"You are?" I whispered.

"Why do you think I've been telling you all summer that I'm so exciting?" he asked. "You were oblivious of me. I'm not exactly good-looking."

I shook my head. "You are devastatingly handsome," I said and smiled.

I wished we could have stood there talking like that forever, it was so dramatic, but I was shivering. When the sun goes down in Seattle, it cools off fast. Ferguson took off his jacket and wrapped it around me. Then he put his arm around me, and I put mine around him, and we walked back to the cafeteria.

The band was just starting a slow song. "Let's dance," Ferguson said, taking my hand. We danced very close together, moving to he throbbing rhythm. Ferguson's heart beat against me. I closed my eyes and felt dizzy pleasure as his lips touched my neck and ear. This was the most dramatic situation in the universe, I thought. I would never have dreamed that it would be, but it was.

Ferguson drove me home in his mother's car, and I leaned against him the whole way—it doesn't have bucket seats. We pulled into Ferguson's driveway, and Ferguson turned off the ignition. Neither of us moved.

"Are you going to audition?" Ferguson asked quietly.

"For the school play, I am, but not for *Dracula*. I mean, with a name like MacBeth, I'm bound to get a part, right?"

"Right!"

"And I'm going to join the Karate Club, too," I said. "After tonight, I bet I'm at least a green belt!"

Ferguson walked me to the door and we kissed. I didn't know what I had been so worried about before. Kissing was easy!